KNUT HAMSUN was born in 1859 into a Norwegian farming family. He spent the years of his young manhood wandering from job to job, including two steamer trips to America where he worked as street-car conductor, dairyman, and finally as a fisherman off the Grand Banks of Newfoundland. In 1888 his first novel, HUNGER, was published, establishing him almost immediately as one of the leading Scandinavian writers. During the next few years MYSTERIES, PAN, and VICTORIA (all available in Bard editions) followed. His later novels include WITH MUTED STRINGS, THE WOMEN AT THE PUMP, and THE GROWTH OF THE SOIL, for which Hamsun received the Nobel Prize in 1920. Until his death in 1952, Hamsun lived near Grimstad, in southern Norway, where he wrote and farmed.

HUNGER

KNUT HAMSUN

Translated from the Norwegian by
ROBERT BLY

With Introductions by
ROBERT BLY and ISAAC BASHEVIS SINGER

 BARD BOOKS/PUBLISHED BY AVON

Newly translated from the Norwegian by Robert Bly

AVON BOOKS
A division of
The Hearst Corporation
959 Eighth Avenue
New York, New York 10019

ISBN: 0-380-00556-5

First Bard Printing, December, 1975

BARD TRADEMARK REG. U.S. PAT. OFF. AND
FOREIGN COUNTRIES, REGISTERED TRADEMARK—
MARCA REGISTRADA, HECHO EN CHICAGO, U.S.A.

Printed in the U.S.A.

Introduction by
Isaac Bashevis Singer

KNUT HAMSUN, ARTIST OF SKEPTICISM

WRITERS who are truly original do not set out to fabricate new forms of expression, or to invent themes merely for the sake of appearing new. They attain their originality through extraordinary sincerity, by daring to give everything of themselves, their most secret thoughts and idiosyncrasies. Knut Hamsun's genius is totally a product of self-searching and introspection. This became immediately apparent in his first novel, *Hunger*. People do not love alike; neither do they starve alike. It is interesting to note that although *Hunger* was published during a time of social upheaval and revolutionary propaganda, none of the reformers seized upon it as support for their claims and demands. Those who are so fond of stressing the poverty of the masses detected in this work an almost inimical element. Knut Hamsun took the basic human experience of hunger and made it such a highly individualistic sensation that everything common dropped away from it. In this sense, he went even further than Dostoevsky. There is a strong resemblance between Hamsun's hero in *Hunger* and Dostoevsky's Raskolnikov in *Crime and Punishment*. Both suffer extreme need. Both are literary neophytes. Both are highly nervous, virtually bordering on madness. Both are spiritual aristocrats. I nearly said Nietz-

5

scheans, although Nietzsche was still a student when Dostoevsky wrote his classic.

But, for all their similarity, the two heroes are fundamentally different. Raskolnikov is a man deeply rooted in Russia and matters Russian. Dostoevsky gave a thorough picture of Raskolnikov's mother, of his sister and her groom, of Raskolnikov's friend Rasumihin, along with a whole array of true Russian types and characters. Dostoevsky portrayed the society that produced a Raskolnikov. In Hamsun's work we see the city of Christiania; we feel its physical and spiritual climate; Hamsun mentions names of streets and buildings, but at the same time the reader realizes that the hero is as far removed from his surroundings as if he were in a foreign land. His hunger can be said to be entirely antisocial. He is starving, not because he cannot find a job in the city or on the farm, but mainly because he is obstinately determined to live from his writing although he is just a beginner. He is hungry both for bread and for inspiration. He is lonely, not because he cannot make friends, but because he has no patience for others. He suffers the shame of those who must rise above their fellow creatures or perish.

It is characteristic that when Raskolnikov reminds the investigating prosecutor of the possibility of his escaping from Russia, the prosecutor points out that people like Raskolnikov do not escape. Raskolnikov is tied to Russia. Hamsun's hero, on the other hand, ends by signing on as a crewman on a freighter bound for the seven seas. (Hamsun himself visited America twice in the 1880's and worked as a farmhand in North Dakota and as a streetcar conductor in Chicago. He even wrote a book at that time, *The Cultural Life of Modern America,* in which he sharply vilified this country. In later years he recanted his views.) Raskolnikov is finally redeemed by entering upon a term of penal servitude in Siberia accompanied by his beloved, Sonia, and in a spirit of religious resurrection. Hamsun's hero is, in substance, a suicide, although he does not actually kill himself. Raskolnikov seeks a reckoning with God, while Hamsun's heroes wrangle with fate. In a sense, the hero of *Hunger* wages a hunger strike against destiny.

6

He seems to say: "Either give me inspiration or I'll take my life and frustrate your schemes. . . ." But destiny neither provides him with the inspiration nor allows him to die. He is constantly saved by some temporary deliverance. An editor prints an article or a sketch and the hero is paid a few kroner. Then the ordeal begins all over again. . . .

The suicidal character of Hamsun's hero—all the heroes of his earlier novels are one and the same person—comes out in his masterpiece, *Pan*. Lieutenant Glahn in *Pan* is as lonely as the hero of *Hunger*. Glahn has settled somewhere in a hamlet at the edge of a forest in northern Norway without any practical purpose—simply to be alone. He eats only what he can shoot with his gun. He has no friends besides his dog, Esop. He talks to himself, to the dog, to the trees, and to the sea. He lives in a kind of pantheistic exultation that can go over at any moment into depression. In fact, he exists in a state of perpetual despair. His God, nature, is indifferent, neutral toward good and evil, and frequently cruel. One speaks to it, but it remains silent. Its acts are ambiguous and therefore meaningless. When Glahn falls in love with Edvarda, the young daughter of the merchant Mack, this love is doomed from the start. Knut Hamsun is a master at describing both great love and the contrariness that often accompanies it. Glahn and Edvarda wage a sexual war. The ambition of each is to drive the other insane. The novel ends with Glahn committing suicide in India.

Fictional heroes who are estranged from their environment seldom emerge lifelike. With most writers, such heroes are mere shadows, or, at best, symbols. But Hamsun is able to portray both the environment and the alienation, the soil and the extirpation. His heroes have roots even though they cannot be seen. The reader never knows precisely how they have become what they are, but their existence is real all the same. Hamsun's favorite hero is a young man in his late twenties or early thirties, rash, good-natured, with no plans for the future, always anticipating some happy chance, yet at the same time resigned and melancholy. While Dostoevsky's heroes beat their breasts and seek solutions for themselves and for mankind, Hamsun's hero is frivolous in word and deed. He speaks to people as he would to a dog or to himself.

Hamsun is less popular in the United States than in Europe, but European writers know that he is the father of the modern school of literature in his every aspect—his subjectiveness, his fragmentariness, his use of flashbacks, his lyricism. The whole modern school of fiction in the twentieth century stems from Hamsun, just as Russian literature in the nineteenth century "came out of Gogol's greatcoat." They were all Hamsun's disciples: Thomas Mann and Arthur Schnitzler, Jacob Wassermann and Stefan Zweig, Zeromski and Bunin, Kellermann and Peter Altenberg, D'Annunzio and Hermann Bang, and even such American writers as Fitzgerald and Hemingway, whether they acknowledged the debt or not. Literary influences often do not come in a direct fashion. Hamsun even had an effect on Hebrew and Yiddish literature. Agnon, Schoffmann, and Bergelson were influenced by him. This writer was enchanted with Hamsun's prose for years. Hamsun was perhaps the first to show how childish the so-called grown-ups are. His heroes are all children—as romantic as children, as irrational and often as savage. Hamsun discovered even before Freud did that love and sex are a child's game. . . .

Hamsun belonged to that select group of writers who not only interested a reader but virtually hypnotized him. In pre-World War I Russia, hosts of readers awaited Hamsun's each new book with impatience. The same held true in Germany, Poland, and in all of north, east, and central Europe. Few writers were as imitated as Hamsun. The novel *Ingeborg* by the German writer Kellermann is virtually a copy of *Pan*. Kellermann had been bewitched by Hamsun.

There were a number of reasons why Hamsun's star waned, as the saying goes. To begin with, he lived too long. It would have been better for him artistically had he flared and gone out, as Byron did. But Hamsun lived past ninety and wrote almost to the very end. It may sound like a paradox, but the novel that won him the Nobel Prize, *Growth of the Soil,* marked the beginning of his literary decline. Hamsun himself had grown disgusted with Hamsunism. He attempted to become an epical rather than a lyric writer. He was only partly successful in *Growth of the Soil*. Everything that followed, *The Women at the Well, The Wanderers,* and other subsequent works, were uneven blends of stale romanticism and meager naturalism. Hamsun's literary output of the twenties disappointed his admirers and probably him as well.

The second reason was the violent social changes brought about by the two world wars. Hamsun was not the writer for champions of social justice. They sensed within him the eternal pessimist, the scoffer and profaner. During World War II, the eighty-year-old Hamsun was guilty of a most tragic mistake. Nazi critics read into Hamsun, as they had into Nietzsche, support for their ideologies, and Hamsun deceived himself into thinking that Nazism would spell the end of the left-wing radicalism which repelled him. The Knut Hamsun who had kept aloof of the masses and social reformers allowed himself to be taken in by Nazi demagogues. It was a sad day for many of Hamsun's followers when a picture of him greeting Hitler appeared in the newspapers. In it, Hamsun's face reflects shame, while Hitler looks at him mockingly. In Norway, where strong opposition to Hamsun had always existed due to his isolation and his popularity with foreigners, he was quite properly anathematized. Following Hitler's defeat, Hamsun's sons were imprisoned.

But the literary and political errors of his latter years cannot erase Hamsun's colossal role in the literature of the twentieth century, even though he actually wrote his best works in the nineteenth century: *Hunger* in 1890; *Mysteries* in 1892; *Editor Lynge* in 1893; *Pan* in 1894; and *Victoria* in 1898. (In the intervening years, he published a number of plays.) His novels *Benoni* and *Rosa,* published in 1908, were nothing more than variations of *Pan*. Hamsun received the Nobel Prize in 1920. It is characteristic that upon learning of his prize Hamsun remarked that he would use the money to improve his flower garden. The author of *Hunger* wasn't overly concerned about those who were starving because of conditions in postwar Europe.

Was Knut Hamsun's career nothing more than a great literary quirk? Far from it! All that is genuine has roots. Hamsun was deeply rooted in his country and in Scandinavian culture. But, like many other masters, he was a man before his time. His skepticism, or perhaps it could be called Pyrrhonism—doubting even the doubts—belonged to a later era. To Hamsun, man was nothing but a chain of moods that kept constantly changing, often without a trace of consistency. Man was, therefore, as strong as his weakest mood. The hero of *Hunger* doubted the existence of God, yet he prayed to Him. He loved, but he belittled this love and all that it stood for. He strove for artistic revelation, yet wasn't really serious in his approach to art. Doubt, not only the philosophical but the mundane, found in Hamsun its narrator par excellence.

Because he was responsible for a whole school of writing, Hamsun cannot appear as fresh today as he did when he literally stunned Europe with his content and his style. But it can be positively stated that none of his disciples has surpassed him. This is particularly true of his two classics, *Hunger* and *Pan*. It is a good thing that this new edition of *Hunger*, in an excellent retranslation by Robert Bly, will now be available, so that American readers will have the opportunity to discover who originated the prose of our time. It is not Hamsun's fault, as it wasn't Byron's, that he inspired a virtual chorus of imitators who muddled his literary achievements. It is almost axiomatic that the more original a writer is, the more he is mimicked. Both Byron and Hamsun transformed skepticism into art. Both expressed the futility of a life that is blind, of a hope without faith, of a fight without purpose. Both were masters at portraying the abyss of the human emotions.

New York City
April 1967

Introduction by
Robert Bly

THE ART OF HUNGER

ONE reason *Hunger* is powerful is that it compresses into a few months ten years of genuine and desperate life. Hamsun's ten years of starvation and physical labor were, in their effect, like Dostoevsky's term in the Siberian prison: the experience drove him harshly into himself, intensified his imagination, and made him more than just a "writer." It forced him to be inward. During those ten years, Hamsun never got a job among "educated people." Such jobs, like teaching jobs in the United States, mean that the writer is working with people "he can talk to." Since Hamsun was never with those people, he learned instead to talk to himself. Antonio Machado, the Spanish poet, said that the writer should listen to himself, and "ought to overtake by surprise some of the phrases of his inward conversations with himself, distinguishing the living voice from the dead echoes." Hamsun realized all this: in his preface to *The Cultural Life of Modern America,* he said, "Truth telling does not involve seeing both sides or objectivity; truth telling is unselfish inwardness" (*uegennyttige Subjectivitet*).

In *Hunger,* Hamsun was participating in a general turn toward inwardness in European thought at the end of the nineteenth century: Kierkegaard took part in that movement also, as did the Danish novelist Jens Peter Jacobsen,

11

whose work Rilke loved so much. Like Jacobsen and Kierkegaard, Hamsun turned inward with great determination. *Hunger* was prepared for by hour after hour, year after year of keeping watch on the moods rising and falling in his mind. An idea or an impulse rises above the horizon like a moon: Hamsun watches its whole course carefully, like an inward astronomer, convinced we have been too casual in watching the movements of the "heavenly bodies" or demonic bodies inside.

He watches with immense care. Our better novelists show vividly how their characters' thoughts make, over a half-hour period, curious loops and unexpected turns. But Hamsun is able to draw such a map for a *minute* of his character's time. He has a magnifying glass on his eye, like a jeweler's. The reader is constantly astounded by the precise detail with which we come to know the character's intelligence, and also by the intensity of that intelligence.

How few books there are today in which a genius is the main character! Fewer and fewer, as serious novelists more and more tend to put people of lower intelligence than themselves into books, so that the readers will feel at home. Hamsun disdains such a practice. To have the hero of your work the most intelligent person you can imagine is more a Greek than a Christian idea. The Greeks liked heroes with great strength of personality and vigorous intelligence. *Hunger* shares with the ancient tragedies and much ancient poetry another Greek quality—a curious joyfulness. It's odd to suggest that a book named *Hunger* is essentially a joyful book, but it is true. The mood of the prose is delight: a delight in watching the intelligence, particularly the tendency of the intelligence to *play*, even in deep crisis.

Hunger shocked many readers, and still does, because Hamsun does not resort to rhetoric or hysteria when he catches sight of demonic impulses. The more orthodox Western attitude toward the demonic, in which both Billy Graham and William Burroughs in differing ways are trapped, responds to anything demonic with hysteria. Hamsun watches a cruel impulse come forward—for example, the desire to save face that ends his character's conversation with the street whore in Part Three—and he neither becomes moralistic like the orthodox religionist nor does he lick his lips hungrily as the de Sade disciples do, but rather looks at the impulse calmly, even affectionately. His calmness, like that of the old Zen teacher, suggests that all this hysteria about the impulses is senseless and unintelligent: the essence of right life is this—when you are hungry, eat; when you are tired, sleep. The book then is morally at odds with a great deal of Western literature, and it is incompatible with most European moral literature. *Hunger* blew much moralistic work of the time, like Ibsen's, apart.

Hamsun liked to blow things apart. A new sort of art can, of course, without fuss simply push an older art into the background. Eliot's *Waste Land* made Browning's work appear invalid, though Eliot never himself attacked Browning. Hamsun, however, attacked his artistic elders in person. Shortly after he published *Hunger*, and while he was still relatively unknown, he embarked on a lecture tour of Norway. The country had four national literary heroes: Bjørnstjerne Bjørnson, Alexander Kielland, Jonas Lie, and Henrik Ibsen. They were loved like Robert Frost or Marianne Moore in America—more so; clouds of national pride hung around them. Hamsun disregarded the national pride—he bored into the sentimental and contradictory ideas of Bjørnson, and attacked the foggy and vague art of Jonas Lie and Kielland. Word of his offensive lectures spread. At his last stop, in Oslo, Henrik Ibsen, recently returned after twenty-some years in southern Europe, was sitting in the front row, glaring. Hamsun did not hesitate, but finished Ibsen off in the same style. He mocked Ibsen's moral preachiness, and his argumentative drama, which Hamsun thought was far inferior to true psychological drama, and he attacked Ibsen for creating characters that had an intelligence no higher than his audience.

Ibsen's play, *The Master Builder*, written soon after, grew I think out of that painful hour with Hamsun. Ibsen talks there of a new architect who is challenging the old

13

poorly educated master builder. Ibsen's hero admits that he has perhaps built too many "homes for ordinary people"; perhaps he had made a mistake in not building more "cathedrals."

In these terms, *Hunger* is a cathedral. It is a cathedral because the whole novel is a resonating chamber for an unknown part of the personality.

Knut Hamsun was born August 4, 1859, as Knut Petersen, in the Gudbransdal valley of central Norway. Gudbransdal farmers, from which he came, were traditionally stubborn and self-willed. His mother's family went back to some nobility of the late Middle Ages; his father, Peter Petersen Skultbakken, farmed, but was romantic in temperament, and liked to travel. When Knut was four, the family decided to go to the far north; they settled on a farm in Hamaroy named Hamsund, whose name Hamsun later took as his own. Knut Petersen as a boy herded cattle through the long ecstatic northern nights lit up by the Arctic sun, and learned to love roaming about alone. He avoided school, and from the age of fourteen he was on his own, helping shoemakers or sheriffs. When he was twenty, he wrote a novella called *Frida* and then went to Oslo (at the time called Christiania) himself to offer it to the great publishing house, Gyldendal. They refused it. Hamsun decided to appeal the verdict. Ibsen was living in Italy, so he went to see Bjørnson, the other great Norwegian writer, and brought him the story.

We know how this scene in a famous writer's life is supposed to go: the older man recognizes the younger writer's genius, encourages him, fights for him, and helps him get some sort of teaching or editing job. But Hamsun had a surprise at Bjørnson's house. Bjørnson read his novella and advised him to become an actor.

Hamsun was now twenty-one, and a ten-year stretch of starvation and physical labor lay ahead before his first novel would be published. He slid into his period of starvation shortly after seeing Bjørnson; he spent the winter of 1879–80 in extreme poverty in the poor section of Oslo, in the rooming house described in the last part of *Hunger*.

That spring, he escaped from Christiania by taking a job as a road laborer, but the escape merely set the pattern: starvation, then physical labor. Ibsen by contrast was a university man; soon after graduation, a theater hired him as a director. Through the period of his artistic development, the middle class offered him help, which he accepted. Hamsun's life was harder and he owed nothing to the middle class, even for staying alive. When he was twenty-three, he left Norway for America, where he worked first at Elroy, Wisconsin, and later at a lumberyard in Madelia, Minnesota. A Unitarian minister tried to make a preacher of him, but that didn't work. One day in Minneapolis, after he had been in the United States for two years, as he was just finishing a hard day's work as an auctioneer, he suddenly began to spit blood. The doctor's diagnosis was terminal tuberculosis, with three months to live. His friends chipped in with money for the ship fare back to Norway; Hamsun meanwhile decided to cure himself. He took a train to New York, and in his eccentric way rode on top of the locomotive the whole trip, with his mouth open. He gulped down huge quantities of fresh air. By the time he got to New York, three days later, he declared himself half cured already. We recognize the willful hero of *Hunger*. He did return to Norway from New York, and had no more trouble from the disease.

But a second period of starvation in Christiania began. He went to see the writer Arne Garborg this time. Same luck. He starved in the city again, selling an article here or there. Many of the incidents from the spring and summer of 1886 went into *Hunger*. In the fall, he saw it was hopeless and went back to the United States. This time he worked as a streetcar conductor in Chicago and spent a summer working in the wheat fields of North Dakota. After two years more in the United States, he decided to start cutting hair to get money for a return to Europe. He finally got back to Copenhagen in the summer of 1888, with at least some of *Hunger* written. The next year he published a fierce and fantastic book on the United States, very funny in parts, called *The Cultural*

Life of Modern America. At last, in 1890, when he was thirty-one, his first novel, *Hunger,* came out.

The swiftness and pungency of the prose astounded everyone. It made Norwegian seem like a young language. Hamsun had worked hard to get that swiftness. There are many reports from the United States of his writing all night and then at dawn ripping up everything he had written and jumping on it, or throwing it out the window. And the United States probably contributed something to the newness of the style. The Norwegian novelist Sigurd Hoel said he thought the excitability, the constant slang, and the sarcasm of American talk had a lot to do with *Hunger's* style. In Norwegian, the sentences are abrupt, swift, and graceful, curiously like the best of Hemingway. Some thirty years later, Hemingway's short and pungent sentences startled American readers used to the long sentences of Dickens and Henry James.

We notice that *Hunger* has one other quality that reminds us of a Hemingway novel: it is not a book of social protest. It is not a cry against a society that will allow the kind of poverty we see throughout the book. The reason in Hamsun's case is simple. He does not have faith enough in the middle class even to make a proposal to it. By contrast, Zola actually trusted the middle class even as he attacked it: he thought that if an injustice was pointed out clearly, the middle class would correct it. Hamsun's experience with the middle class as a youth had taught him, as similar experiences taught W. C. Fields, that the bourgeoisie could not be trusted. As an adult, he saw it as the killer of the impulsive and exuberant life he believed in.

After *Hunger,* Hamsun's life was not so difficult. He published novel after novel, and was soon able to live on his royalties. When he was thirty-nine, he married a Norwegian woman he had taken away from her rich Austrian husband. They were divorced seven years later. When he was fifty, he married a Norwegian actress, and wrote a book called *A Wanderer Plays on Muted Strings When He Is Fifty.* He changed his way of life again. He moved back to the far north, and built up a farm, doing much of the physical work himself. Later he bought a former nobleman's expensive estate much nearer Oslo, and lived on that estate for thirty-four years, until his death in 1952 at the age of ninety-three. At ninety he wrote his last book, his prose still swift, intense, and collected.

One interesting faith runs through all of *Hunger*—a curious, almost superstitious faith in the unconscious. The main character listens a great deal "with his antennae." He senses the woman in black under the street lamp is linked to him even before he talks to her. He is sure the word "Cisler" is a sign to him from "higher powers." He obeys his impulses instantly, showing an unusually open avenue between his unconscious and his consciousness, no matter if it is an impulse to bite his own finger (which pulls him out of a serious daze), or the impulse to hire a taxi and drive off to a nonexistent address, or the impulse to speak to strangers. He takes great delight in obeying these impulses.

The main character of *Hunger* feels no pity for himself, and we do not, because there is a sense throughout the entire novel that his starvation was somehow planned by his unconscious—that somehow his unconscious has chosen this suffering as a way for some part of him to get well. The hero of *Hunger* obeys the unconscious, and remains in hunger, despite suffering, until he has lived through what he must, or learned what he had to. What seems to us catastrophe, his spirit experiences as secret victory. His anarchic inability to support himself is experienced by his spirit as obedience. What seems to the careless observer a series of sordid collapses appears to his spirit as a series of ascetic exultations, in each of which some tiny filaments holding the personality to its past shell are separated. His obedience to the unconscious, even at the cost of physical suffering, is the right thing; it is the road of genius and of learning. His painful starvation has called up an immense reserve of healing power that had been lying concealed in the psyche. Blake wrote: "The road of excess leads to the palace of wis-

17

dom." "Exuberance is beauty." "If the fool would persist in his folly he would become wise."

When Hamsun's hero has lived through what he must, and has learned what he must, his unconscious loses interest in his hungering and allows him to take a job on the ship, and the book ends. By that time, he has been changed. The hero realizes this on the ship at the end. As he looks back toward Christiania, "where the windows shone with such brightness," he understands that he is now set apart, that he will never be a part of the comfortable domestic life of Europe. Hamsun of course was not his character, and it cannot be said that he himself became wise.

One or two words on translation problems: I have kept throughout to Norwegian money and have not tried to translate the sums into American terms. A krone (plural kroner) is worth about fourteen cents now; an øre is the hundredth part of a krone. In the late nineteenth century, when this novel was written, the krone had more purchasing power than it has now—conceivably to the amount of seventy-five cents or a dollar. Five kroner—an immense sum he constantly longs for—is not very much. Hamsun throughout the novel plays on the grotesque disproportion between the hero's vast works on "Crimes of the Future" or some such subject, and the infinitesimal sums which are paid for them, or hoped for. For his works of genius the hero receives $3 or $3.50. Knut Hamsun doesn't whine about this disproportion—he finds it funny.

In the matter of street names in Christiania, I had the choice of writing, for instance, Vognmandsgaten (*gaten* means "street"), which name the reader might take as a district of the city, not as a street at all; or writing Vognmandsgaten Street, which would be a bit like a German translating our President's name as Herr Mr. Johnson—it's gilding the lily; or writing Vognmands Street. We took the last choice, as the clearest.

A final detail: Wedel-Jarlsberg, the name the hero announces to the frightened girl who has suspected him of being a beggar, is the name of the only Norwegian noble family that survived the Black Death, and continues to persist on into the present. So that name has a special reasonance in Norway. The Norwegians recognize in the sudden appearance of the name an insolent wit characteristic of the book.

Madison, Minnesota
April 1967

PART ONE

ALL of this happened while I was walking around starving in Christiania—that strange city no one escapes from until it has left its mark on him. . . .

I was lying awake in my attic room; a clock struck six somewhere below; it was fairly light already and people were beginning to move up and down the stairs. Over near the door, where my wall was papered with old issues of the *Morning Times,* I could make out a message from the Chief of Lighthouses, and just to the left of that an advertisement for fresh bread, showing a big, fat loaf: Fabian Olsen's bakery.

As soon as I was wide awake, I took to thinking, as I always did, if I had anything to be cheerful about today. Things had been a bit tight for me lately; one after the other of my possessions had been taken to my "uncle" at the pawnshop; I was becoming more and more nervous and irritable, and several mornings lately I had been so dizzy I had had to stay in bed all day. Occasionally when my luck was good I took in five kroner or so from one of the newspapers for an article.

It was getting lighter, and I concentrated on the advertisements by the door; I could even read the slim, mocking typeface declaring: "Shrouds available, Miss Andersen, Main Entrance, to the right." That satisfied me for a long time. The clock below had struck eight before I got up and dressed.

I opened the window and looked out. I could see a clothesline and an open field. Behind them there was some debris from a burned-down blacksmith's shop which the workmen were just now cleaning away. Leaning my elbows on the windowsill, I gazed up into the sky. Today would be clear. The fall had come, that cool and delicious time of year when everything changed color and died. Noises were floating up from the streets, tempting me to go out. This empty room whose floor gave a little with every step was like a badly put-together coffin; the room had no real lock, and no stove; I usually slept on my socks so they would be a little drier by morning. The only nice thing in the room was a small red rocking chair in which I sat in the evenings, and dozed and thought about all sorts of things. When the wind was strong, and the street door of the house had been left open, all kinds of weird whines would come through the floor, and out of the walls, and the *Morning Times* by the door would get tears in it as long as a hand.

I stood up and investigated a little bundle I had over in the corner by the bed, looking for something for breakfast, but found nothing and went back again to the window.

I thought, God only knows if there's any sense in my looking for a job any longer! All these refusals, these partial promises, simple noes, hopes built up and knocked down, new tries that ended each time in nothing—these had squashed my courage for good. The last time, I had tried for a job as a bill collector, but arrived too late; I couldn't have got together fifty kroner for a bond anyway. There was always one thing or another in the way. I had even tried to join the Fire Department. A half hundred of us stood there in the entryway, sticking our chests out to give the impression of strength and tremendous audacity. A captain walked around inspecting these applicants, felt their muscles, and asked a question or two. He merely shook his head as he walked past me, and said I was out because of my glasses. I turned up again, later, without the glasses. I stood there with my eyebrows scrunched up, and made my eyes as sharp as knife ends: he walked past me again, and smiled—he had recognized me. The worst of it was that my clothes were beginning to look so bad I couldn't really present myself any longer for a job that required someone respectable.

How steadily my predicament had gotten worse! By now I was so utterly denuded of objects that I didn't even have a comb left, or a book to read when I felt hopeless. I had spent the entire summer sitting in cemeteries or in the public gardens near the castle, writing articles intended for some newspaper: page after page on almost any subject, filled with odd ideas, inspirations, quirks rising from my restless brain. In desperation I would choose the most outré subjects; the pieces would cost me hours and hours of labor, and were never accepted. When a piece was done I plunged immediately into a new one, and therefore wasn't very often crushed by an editor's refusal; I told myself all the time that eventually my luck would turn. And in fact, sometimes when I had luck, and things were going my way, I could get five kroner for one afternoon's work.

I stood up from the window again, went over to the washstand and sprinkled some water on my shiny trousers to make them look blacker and newer. When I had finished that, I put paper and pencil in my pocket as usual and went out. I slipped down the stairs very quietly so as not to attract my landlady's attention; my rent had been due a few days ago and I had nothing to pay her with at the moment.

It was nine. The rattle of wagons and the hum of voices filled the air—growing into a great orchestra of sound into which the noise of people walking and the cracks of the drivers' whips fit perfectly. The traffic noise on all sides cheered me up immediately, and I began to feel more content and at peace. I had much more to do of course than merely to take a morning stroll in the fresh air. What did my lungs care for fresh air? I was powerful as a giant and could stop a wagon with my shoulders. A rare and delicate mood, a feeling of wonderful lightheartedness had taken hold of me. I began examining the people I met or passed, I read the posters on walls, noticed a glance thrown at me from a streetcar, let every trivial occurrence influence me, every tiny detail that crossed my eyes and vanished.

If one only had something to eat, just a little, on such a clear day! The mood of the gay morning overwhelmed me, I became unusually serene, and started to hum for pure joy and for no particular reason. In front of a butcher's shop there was a woman with a basket on her arm, debating about some sausage for dinner; as I went past, she looked up at me. She had only a single tooth in the lower jaw. In the nervous and excitable state I was in, her face made an instant and revolting impression on me—the long yellow tooth looked like a finger sticking out of her jaw, and as she turned toward me, her eyes were still full of sausage. I lost my appetite instantly, and felt nauseated. When I came to the main market square, I went over to the fountain and drank a little water. I looked up: ten o'clock by the Church of Our Saviour.

I kept on going through streets, rambling on with no purpose in mind at all. I stopped at a corner without needing to, turned and went up small alleys without having anything to do there. I just drifted on, floating in the joyful morning, rolling along without a care among other happy people. The air was clear and bright and my mind was without a shadow.

For the last ten minutes an old man had been limping ahead of me. He had a bundle in one hand, and was using his entire body to move forward, working with all his strength and yet making very little progress. I could hear him puffing from the effort. It occurred to me that I might carry his bundle; but I made no attempt to overtake him. On Grænsen Street I met Hans Pauli, who said hello and hurried by. Why should he be in such a hurry? I certainly didn't plan to ask him for money; in fact I wanted first of all to return to him a blanket I'd borrowed from him a few weeks ago. As soon as I was in better shape I would; the last thing I wanted was to owe a man a blanket; perhaps today, as a matter of fact, I would get

24

an article started on "Crimes of the Future" or "Freedom of the Will," something like that, something salable enough so I could get five kroner at least. . . . Thinking about the article, I suddenly felt a strong desire to work on it immediately, and drain off my mind. I'd find a good spot in the public gardens and keep on until I had the whole thing done.

However, the old cripple was still making the same wiggly movements ahead of me in the street. Finally it began to irritate me to have this feeble creature in front of me all the time. His journey evidently had no end; maybe he was determined to go to exactly the same place as I and I would have him blocking my view the whole way. In my excited condition I had become convinced that at each crossing he had hesitated, as though waiting to see what direction I would take, and then had taken a stronger hold on his bundle and limped off with all his might to get a head start. I walked on, looking at this tedious creature, and became more and more full of rage at him; it was clear he was destroying my good spirits bit by bit, little by little dragging the pure and magnificent morning down to his own ugliness. He looked like a huge humping insect determined to make a place for himself in the world by force and violence and keep the sidewalk all to himself. By the time we got to the top of the hill, I wanted no more part of it; I stopped in front of a shop window, and waited till he had time to get away; but when I started off again after a few minutes, the man cropped up in front of me again: he must have stopped also. Without thinking, I took three or four quick steps, caught up with him, and slapped him on the shoulder.

He stopped short. We began staring at each other.

"Can you give me a little something for a glass of milk?" he said at last, and let his head fall to the side.

Now there was no turning back! I fumbled in my pockets and said, "Oh, yes, milk. Hmm. Money isn't easy to get these days, and I'm not sure how much you really need it."

"I haven't eaten a thing since yesterday in Drammen,"

the man said. "I don't have an øre and I still can't find work."

"What do you do?"

"I'm a welt binder."

"A what?"

"Welt binder. I can also make the whole shoe."

"Well, that's different," I said. "Wait here a few minutes, and I'll see if I can't find something for you, a little something at least."

I ran down Pile Street, where I knew of a pawnshop on the second floor; it was one I had never been to either. As I went in the main entrance I quickly slipped off my waistcoat, rolled it up and put it under my arm; then I went up the stairs and knocked on the door. I bowed and threw the waistcoat down on the counter.

"One and a half kroner," said the man.

"Very good," I answered. "If it hadn't begun to be a little too tight for me, I don't know how I could have parted with it."

I took the money and went back. Actually, pawning this waistcoat was a wonderful idea; I would still have money left over for a good fat breakfast, and by evening my piece on "Crimes of the Future" would be in shape. Life began immediately to seem more friendly, and I hurried back to the man to get him off my hands.

"Here you go," I said, giving him one of my coins. "I'm delighted that you came to me first."

The man took the money and began to look me up and down. What was he standing there staring at? I got the sensation that he was inspecting my trousers particularly, and I became irritated at this impertinence. Did this old fool imagine I was really as poor as I looked? Hadn't I just as good as begun my ten-kroner article? On the whole, I had no fears for the future; I had many irons in the fire. What business was it of this heathen savage if I helped him out on such a marvelous day? The man's stare irritated me, and I decided to give him a little lesson before I let him go. I threw back my shoulders and said, "My dear man, you have gotten into a very bad habit, namely, staring at a man's knees after he gives you money."

His head settled back against the wall, and his mouth fell open. Behind the idiotic forehead something was going on, he had concluded that I was trying to trick him in some way and he handed the money back.

I stamped my foot, swore, and told him to keep it. Did he think I intended to go to all this trouble for nothing? When you came down to it, I probably owed him the money, I just happened to remember an old debt, he was looking at a punctilious man, one honorable right down to his fingernails. In short, the money was his. . . . Nonsense, nothing to thank me for, it was a pleasure. Goodbye.

I walked off. At last I was rid of this painful pest, and could be undisturbed. I went back up Pile Street and stopped in front of a grocery. The window was crammed with food, and I decided to go in and get something to take along.

"Some cheese and a French loaf!" I said, and threw my half krone down on the counter.

"All of this is to go for bread and cheese?" the woman asked in an ironic tone, without looking at me.

"The entire fifty øre," I replied, not at all upset.

I took my bundles, said good morning with the most exquisite politeness to the old fat woman, and started off at full speed toward the castle and the public gardens. I found a bench to myself and began chewing savagely at my lunch. It did me good; it had been a long time since I'd had such a well-balanced meal and I gradually became aware of the same feeling of tired peace which one feels after a long cry. My courage had now returned; it was not enough any longer to write an essay on something so elementary and simple-minded as "Crimes of the Future," which any ass could arrive at, let alone read in history books. I felt ready for a more difficult enterprise, I was in the mood to conquer obstacles and I determined on a consideration in three parts of Philosophical Consciousness. Naturally I'd find a moment to break the neck of some of Kant's sophistries. . . . When I reached to take my writing materials to begin work, I discovered that my pencil was gone—I had forgotten and left it in the pawnshop: my pencil was still in the waistcoat pocket.

God, how eager everything was to go wrong around me! I swore several times, leaped up from the bench, and strolled back and forth on the path. Everything was silent; near the queen's summerhouse two nursemaids were wheeling their baby carriages along; otherwise, not a person was to be seen anywhere. I was profoundly bitter, and strolled up and down in front of my bench like a maniac. How amazingly everything fell to pieces on all sides! An essay in three parts left high and dry for no reason than that there was missing from my pocket a ten-øre pencil! Suppose I went down to Pile Street again and got the pencil back? There would still be time to get a lot done before the mob would come and fill the park. Moreover, there was so much at stake with this investigation of Philosophical Consciousness, perhaps the happiness of many persons. Who could tell? I told myself that the piece could very well be a great help for dozens of young people. Actually, I wouldn't attack Kant after all, I could avoid that, I would just have to make an invisible detour when I came to the problem of Space and Time; but Renan would have to take care of himself, Renan, that old preacher. . . . In any case, what was essential was an article of so and so many pages; the unpaid room rent and the landlady's long look in the morning when I met her on the stairs bothered me all day and even cropped up in my gay moods when I hadn't another dark thought in my head. This would have to come to an end. I walked rapidly out of the park to get my pencil from the pawnshop.

At the bottom of the hill I overtook and passed two women. As I walked by them, I brushed the arm of one. I looked up; she had a plump, slightly pale face. All at once she blushed and became wonderfully beautiful—I don't know the reason; perhaps from a word she had heard from someone passing, perhaps because of some silent thought inside her. Or was it because I had touched her arm? Her full bosom heaved noticeably several times, and she clenched her hands firmly on her parasol, handle. What was she thinking?

I stopped and allowed her to go on ahead; actually at that moment I couldn't have gone farther anyway, the entire series of events seemed to me so curious. I was in an excitable mood, angry with myself for the business with the pencil, and extremely stimulated by all the food just eaten on an empty stomach. Suddenly my thoughts shot off on a lunatic direction, and I felt myself possessed by a strange desire to frighten this woman, to follow her and hurt her in some way or other. I caught up again and walked past, then abruptly turned and looked back at her to study her. I stopped and stared at her face to face, and on the spot a name came to me I'd never heard before, a name with a smooth, nervous sound: Ylayali. When she was very close, I drew myself up straight and said in an impressive voice, "Miss, you are losing your book."

I could hear my heart thump audibly as I said that.

"My book?" she said to her companion. She walked on.

My malice increased and I followed the two. I was conscious all the time that I was following mad whims without being able to do anything about it. My deranged consciousness ran away with me and sent me lunatic inspirations, which I obeyed one after the other. No matter how much I told myself that I was acting idiotically, it did not help; I made the most stupid faces behind the women's backs, and I coughed furiously several times as I went by them. Walking on in this way, very slowly, always a few steps ahead, I could feel her eyes on my back, and I bowed my head involuntarily in shame at persecuting her. Gradually I began to feel a marvelous sense of being far, far away, in another place entirely; I had a sort of vague conviction that it wasn't I who was walking there on the sidewalk and bowing my head. In a few minutes, the women had reached Pascha's Bookstore. I had already stopped at the first window, and as they went by, I stepped out and said once more, "Miss, you are losing your book."

"Book, what book?" she said in a frightened voice. "Whatever sort of book is he talking about?"

She stopped. I gloated cruelly over her confusion; the bewilderment in her eyes fascinated me. Her thought could not grasp my desperate and petty persecution; she has no book at all with her, not even a page of a book, and yet now she looks through her pockets, gazes repeatedly at her hands, turns her head and examines the sidewalk behind her, strains her small and tender brain to its limit to find out what sort of book I am talking about. Her face turns various colors, shows now one and now another expression, and her breath is audible; even the buttons on her dress seem to stare at me like a row of alarmed eyes.

"Don't bother with him," her friend said, and took her arm. "He's drunk—don't you see how drunk he is!"

Despite my alienation from myself at that moment, and even though I was nothing but a battleground for invisible forces, I was aware of every detail of what was going on around me. A big brown dog ran across the street, toward the trees and the Tivoli; it had a small collar made of Mexican silver. Farther up the street, a window on the first story opened and a girl with her sleeves rolled up leaned out and began polishing the panes on the outside. Nothing escaped my eyes, I was sharp and my brain was very much alive, everything poured in toward me with a staggering distinctness as if a strong light had fallen on everything around me. The women before me had two blue feathers in their hats, and plaid kerchiefs around their necks. It occurred to me that they were sisters.

They turned in and stopped at Cisler's Music Shop, talking. I stopped also. Then they turned around, returned the same way they had come, passed me once more, turned the corner at University Street, and went up to St. Olaf's Place. I was at their heels, as near as I dared, all the time. They turned once, giving me a half-frightened, half-inquisitive look, and I saw no irritation in their manner, nor any wrinkled brows. This patience with my pestering made me ashamed, and I dropped my eyes. I no longer wanted to torture them, I wanted out of sheer gratitude to keep track of them with my eyes, not lose sight of them until they were safely inside some building.

Outside 2 St. Olaf's Place, a large house with four stories, they stopped once more, and then went in. I leaned against the lamppost near the fountain, and listened for their steps on the stair: the steps died away in the third story. I came in from the lamppost and looked up at the front of the house. Then something odd happened. High up, some curtains moved, an instant later the window opened, a head appeared, and two remarkable eyes rested on me. Ylayali! I said half aloud, and I felt myself turning red. Why didn't she call for help? Why didn't she push one of the flowerpots over on my head or send someone down to chase me away? We stood looking into each other's eyes without moving; this lasted a minute; thoughts shot between the window and the street, and not a word was said. She turned away. I felt something wrenched in me, a delicate shock went through my system; I saw a shoulder which slowly swung about, a back that disappeared into the room. This leisurely turning from the window, and the expression of the shoulder as it turned, was a sign to me. My blood recognized this delicate greeting and at that moment I felt marvelously happy inside. Then I turned and went back down the street.

I didn't dare look back to find out if she had come to the window again: the more I wondered about this, the more restless and excited I became. The chances were she was standing there this instant following all of my movements: I couldn't help knowing that I was being examined in this way from behind. I drew myself up as well as I could and walked on. Small jerks began to appear in my legs, my walk became unsteady precisely because I wanted it to be smooth. In order to seem calm and indifferent I swung my arms pointlessly, spit to the side, and looked up at the sky, but it was no good—I felt the watching eyes on my neck every second and a chill ran through my body. Finally I escaped by turning into a side street, from which I went on down to Pile Street to get my pencil back.

I had no trouble in retrieving it. The man brought me the waistcoat itself and invited me to go through all the pockets. I found a couple of other pawnshop tickets, which I kept, thanking the man for being so obliging. I became more and more taken with him; at that moment it was extremely important for me to make a good impression on this person. I started off toward the door and then turned back to the counter as if I had forgotten something. I felt I owed him an explanation, some sort of reason, and I began to hum in order to attract his attention. Then I took the pencil and held it up in the air.

"It would never have occurred to me," I said, "to go to such trouble for just any pencil; this case is something special: there is a reason. This stump of a pencil may look insignificant, but this pencil is responsible for getting me where I am in the world, it has given me so to speak my position in life. . . ."

I stopped there. The man came all the way over to the counter.

"Is that so?" he said, looking curiously at me.

"With this pencil," I went on straight-faced, "I wrote my great work on the Philosophical Consciousness in three volumes. You have heard of it, I trust?"

It seemed to him that he had heard the name, the title only.

"Yes, that's it! That was mine! So it isn't really surprising if I wanted that tiny stub of a pencil back: it is very precious to me, it is almost a human being to me. In any case, I am tremendously grateful to you for your kindness and I will remember you for it—no, no, I will remember you for it without question: a promise is a promise, that is the sort of man I am, and you certainly have deserved it. Good day."

I strolled to the door, keeping the posture of a man who can place another easily in an important post. The polite pawnbroker bowed twice to me as I went; I turned once more and said good day.

On the stairs I met a woman carrying a suitcase. She

flattened herself against the wall to let me go by since I looked so prepossessing, and I involuntarily reached in my pocket for something to give her. When I found nothing, my pose collapsed, and I passed her with my head bowed. A moment after, I heard her, too, knocking at the pawnbroker's door: the door had a steel grillwork attached to it, and I recognized the reverberations as the knock disturbed it.

The sun was high, the time nearly twelve. The streets were beginning to come alive as the time approached for strolling in the sun. People laughing and nodding flowed up and down Karl Johan Street. I held my elbows near my sides, made myself small, and slipped unobtrusively by some acquaintances who had stationed themselves near the university to admire the passers-by. I strolled up to the Royal Gardens and fell to brooding.

These people I met on the streets, how gaily and lightly they rolled their shining heads and swung through life as if through a ballroom! Not a single eye had grief in it, no shoulders had burdens, in these happy minds there was not a clouded thought, not even a tiny hidden pain. I walked there, alongside these creatures, young myself, hardly leafed out, and I had already forgotten what happiness was! I hugged these thoughts close to me, and found that a terrible injustice had been done to me. Why had these last few months gone so much against me? I could no longer remember my own joyful nature, and I had the strangest troubles coming from all sides. I could not sit on a park bench by myself or put my foot down anywhere without being besieged by tiny and pointless events, absurd nonsense, which forced itself into my brain and scattered my powers to the four winds. A dog that shot past me, a yellow rose in someone's lapel, could set my thoughts in motion and obsess me for hours. What was the matter with me? Had the hand of the Lord reached out and pointed at me? Well then, why me? Why not just as well at some man in South America? When I pondered these things, it semed more and more incomprehensible why precisely I should have been chosen as the guinea pig for a whim of God's favor. It was an extremely odd way of going about things, to leap over the whole human race in order to arrive at me; for example, there was Pascha, the rare-book dealer, and Hennechen, the steamship clerk.

I walked along arguing with myself about these things, and could not stop; I came on the weightiest objections against the Lord's arbitrariness in letting me suffer for everyone else's sins. Even after I had found a bench and sat down, this question remained, occupying my mind and keeping me from any other thought. From that day in May when my setbacks had begun, I could see clearly all the landmarks of a gradually increasing weakness: now I had become too feeble to steer or guide myself, so to speak, where I wanted to go; a cloud of tiny vermin had forced its way inside me and eaten me out hollow. And what if God had decided absolutely to finish me? I stood up and walked back and forth in front of my bench.

My entire being was full of incredible pain at that moment; even my arms ached, and I could hardly stand to carry them in the usual way. I felt a distinct discomfort from my recent large meal also; I was stuffed and over-stimulated and walked to and fro without looking up; the people who walked around me on both sides slipped by like ghosts. Finally, my seat was taken by two gentlemen who lit their cigars and talked loudly; I became furious and was about to order them off, but turned instead and went over to an entirely different area of the park, where I found a new bench. I sat down.

Thoughts of God began to occupy me again. It seemed to me utterly reprehensible of Him to block my way every time I tried for a job and to ruin my chances when it was only daily bread that I was asking for. I had noticed very clearly that every time I went hungry a little too long it was as though my brains simply ran quietly out of my head and left me empty. My head became light and float-ing, I could no longer feel its weight on my shoulders, and I had the sense that my eyes were remaining far too open when I looked at anything.

I sat there on the bench and thought about all this, and became more and more bitter against God for His constant persecutions. If He wanted to draw me nearer to Himself and make me better by pushing me hard and laying obstacles in my path, He was going about it the wrong way, I could assure Him of that. Then I looked up to the sky almost in tears from my defiance and I told Him that, once and for all, silently, inside myself.

Fragments of childhood teachings ran through my mind, I heard the music of the Bible in my ears, and I talked softly to myself, letting my head fall sarcastically to the side. Why should I be troubled for what I would eat, or for what I would drink, or for what I would put on this vile bag of worms which is called my earthly body? Had not the Heavenly Father cared for me as for those creatures who had no place to lay their heads, and had not His hand in His graciousness pointed at His insignificant servant? God had poked His finger down into my nerves and gently, almost without thinking, brought a little confusion among those threads. And God had pulled His finger back, and behold—there were filaments and fine rootlike threads on His finger from the threads of my nerves. And there remained an open hole behind His finger which was the finger of God, and a wound in my brain behind the path of His finger. But after God had touched me with the finger of His hand, He let me be and touched me no more and let nothing evil come upon me. He let me depart in peace and He let me depart with the open hole. And nothing evil will come upon me from God who is the Lord through all Eternity. . . .

Phrases of band music were coming on the wind all the way from the Student's Promenade. So it was after two. I took out my papers to try some writing; as I did so, my book of barber coupons fell out of my pocket. I opened the book and counted the pages: there were six left. Thank God! I said without thinking; now I could still be shaved for several weeks and look decent! My mood instantly changed for the better because of this little property which I still had left; I smoothed the coupons out carefully and stowed the book away in my pocket.

However, I was unable to write. After a couple of lines, nothing more wanted to come; my thoughts were elsewhere and I couldn't pull myself up to the effort. Everything around bothered me and distracted me; everything I saw obsessed me. Some flies and gnats were sitting on my paper and this disturbed me; I breathed on them to make them go, then blew harder and harder, but it did no good. The tiny beasts lowered their behinds, made themselves heavy, and struggled against the wind until their thin legs were bent. They were absolutely not going to leave the place. They would always find something to get hold of, bracing their heels against a comma or an unevenness in the paper, and they intended to stay exactly where they were until they themselves decided it was the right time to go.

These minuscule monsters kept me busy a long time; I crossed my legs and settled down leisurely to watch them. Suddenly one or two high notes of a clarinet drifted up to me from the concert and started my thoughts off in a new direction. Depressed at not being able to do my article, I poked the papers in my pocket and leaned backward over the bench. In this instant, my head was so clear that I could follow the most difficult train of thought without any effort. Lying in this position, letting my eyes float down over my chest and legs, I noticed the tiny leaping movement my feet made every time my heart beat. I sat up partway and gazed down at my feet. At that moment a strange and fantastic mood came over me which I had never felt before—a delicate and wonderful shock ran through all of my nerves as though a stream of light had flowed through them. As I stared at my shoes, I felt as if I had met an old friend, or got back some part of me that had been torn off: a feeling of recognition went through me, tears came to my eyes, and I experienced my shoes as a soft whispering sound coming up toward me. "Getting weak!" I said fiercely to myself and I closed my fists and said, "Getting weak." I was furious with myself for these ridiculous sensations, which had overpowered me even though I was fully conscious of them. I spoke harsh and sensible phrases, and I closed my eyes tightly to get rid of the tears. Then I began, as though I had never seen my shoes before, to study their expression, their mime-like movements when I moved my toes, their shape, and the worn-out leather they had; and I discovered that their wrinkles and their white seams gave them an expression, provided them with a face. Something of my own being had gone over into these shoes, they struck me as being a ghost of my "I," a breathing part of myself. . . .

I sat there and tried to puzzle out these feelings a long time, perhaps an entire hour. A little old man arrived and took up the other end of my bench; as he sat down, he was puffing heavily after his walk, and said: "Ah ya, ya, ya, ya, ya, ya, yaaah!"

The moment I heard his voice, a wind swept through my head, I let shoes remain shoes, and I had the sensation already that the confused state of mind I had just gone through belonged to some time long ago, perhaps a year or two in the past, and was in the process of vanishing entirely from my memory. I settled down to examine the old man.

What was there about him of interest to me? Nothing, not the slightest thing! Only the fact that he was carrying a newspaper, folded, an outdated issue with the classified section showing; evidently something was wrapped in it. I became inquisitive and couldn't take my eyes from that paper; I got the insane idea that this might be a rare issue, perhaps the only one of its kind. My curiosity rose and I began to slide back and forth on my bench. Perhaps it was hiding official papers, dangerous documents stolen from some files. I had the vague impression of the existence of some secret treaty, a plot.

The man sat motionless, thinking. Why didn't he carry his paper like every other man, with the front page showing? What sort of cunning lay behind that? He looked as though he didn't want to let the parcel out of his hands, not for all the money in the world, he didn't even dare trust it to his own pockets. I'd be willing to risk my life that there was something more here than met the eye.

I concentrated. The very fact that it was impossible to penetrate this enigma made me wild with curiosity. I searched my pockets for something to give the man in order to start a conversation with him; I came on my barber coupons but replaced them. Suddenly I decided to be completely shameless; I patted my empty shirt pocket and said, "May I offer you a cigarette?"

No, thank you, the man did not smoke, he had had to quit in order not to make his eyes worse, he was nearly blind. Thank you anyway very much!

How long was it that his eyes had been weak? Was he able to read? Newspapers, for example?

"Not even newspapers, a shame!"

The man turned toward me. Both of his sick eyes had a film, which gave them a glassy appearance; they looked whitish, and made a revolting impression.

"You are not from here?" he asked.

No. Isn't he able even to read the headlines, for example, of that paper he has there?

Just barely. In any case, he could tell right away that I wasn't from here—there was something in my voice that told him. It didn't need to be much: he had very sharp hearing; at night when everyone else was asleep he could hear the people in the next room breathing. . . . "I wanted to ask you, where do you live?"

A lie appeared full-blown in my head. I lied automatically, without looking forward or back, and answered, "On St. Olaf's Place, number 2."

Is that right? The man knew every stone on St. Olaf's Place. There was a fountain there, street lamps, a couple of trees, he remembered it very well. . . . "What was the number of your apartment?"

I stood up; I wanted to get to the bottom of this, driven wild by my notion about the newspaper. I intended to find out the secret, no matter what it cost.

Well, if you're unable to read even a newspaper, I don't see. . . .

"In number 2, did you say?" the man continued, paying no attention to my impatience. "Once I knew every last person in number 2. Whom do you rent from?"

I found a name quickly in order to get this over—invented one on the spot and tossed it out to bring down my tormentor.

"Happolati," I said.

"Oh, yes, Happolati." The man nodded, and had not missed a single syllable in this difficult name.

I looked at him astonished; he sat there very soberly, with a thoughtful air. I had barely finished pronouncing this stupid name, which had popped into my head, and this man was already at home with it and pretending that he had heard it before. Meanwhile, he laid his parcel down on the bench, and I felt my curiosity become unbearable. I saw clearly that there were two greasy spots on the paper.

"Doesn't your landlord work on a ship?" the man asked; his voice had not a trace of irony in it. "I seem to remember that he worked on a ship."

"On a ship? I don't mean to contradict you, but I wonder if the one you know isn't the brother; this one is J. A. Happolati, a businessman."

I figured this would settle his hash, but he kept on.

"They say he's got quite a head on him," the old man said, pushing forward.

"Oh, he is very sharp," I answered. "A tremendous head for business, he sells everything you could imagine: Russian goosedown and chicken feathers, hides, pulpwood, ink . . ."

"Amazing!" the old man broke out. "Is that so?"—very excited.

I was begining to be drawn in. The plot ran away with me, and one lie after the other popped into my head. I sat down again, forgot the newspaper and the rare documents, became enthusiastic, and got into the swing of it. The gullibility of the little dwarf made me reckless; I was going to stuff him full of lies, no matter what happened, and drive him like a knight from the field.

I wondered if he had heard about the electric prayer book that Happolati had invented?

"What was that, an electric—"

"With electric letters that can light up in the dark? A fantastically big operation, a million kroner going into it, factories and printing presses working now, mobs of engineers on contract already. I've heard some hundred men."

"I'm not really surprised," the man replied calmly. That was all he said: he believed every word I had spoken and did not fall over with amazement. This disappointed me a bit; I had hoped to see him dumfounded at my inventions.

I pulled up a couple of other desperate lies, went all the way, dropped the detail that Happolati had been prime minister of Persia for nine years.

"You probably do not really realize what it means to be prime minister of Persia?" I asked. It was greater than being king here, more like being a sultan, if he knew what that involved. Happolati, however, had settled down marvelously in the job and had never taken a false step. And I told him about Ylayali, his daughter, an enchanted creature, a princess who owned three hundred slaves and slept on a bed made of yellow roses; she was the most beautiful being I had ever seen. I had never seen any woman in my life, so help me God, that could begin to compare with her!

"So, she must have been pretty, then, eh?" the old man mumbled with an absent air, looking down at the ground.

Pretty? She was magnificent, that sort of magnificence ought to have been prohibited! Her eyes were as soft as silk, and her arms the color of amber! A simple glance from her was like a kiss from any other woman, and when she spoke my name her voice poured through my veins like wine right into my heart. And why shouldn't she be that beautiful? Who did he think she was, a filing clerk or a receptionist in the Fire Department? She was simply out of a fairy tale, he could take my word for it, she was a masterpiece, divine!

"Yes, I'm sure she was," the man said, a little bewildered.

His composure bored me; I had become excited by the sound of my own voice and spoke in deadly seriousness. The material stolen from secret files, the agreements signed with some foreign power or other, all this I had forgotten entirely; the small flat bundle lay on the bench between us and I hadn't the slightest desire any longer to see what was in it. I was completely taken up with my own stories, strange visions were passing before my eyes, my blood went to my brain, and I was lying as fast as I could.

All at once the man seemed about to leave. He got halfway up and asked, so as not to break it off too abruptly: "This Happolati, if I'm not mistaken, is quite rich now?"

How did this blind and revolting old fool dare to throw about this remarkable name which I had myself created, treating it as though it were just an ordinary name, plastered on the front of every grocery in town? He never stumbled over a single consonant and never omitted a syllable; this name had sunk deep into his brain and put down roots instantly. I became annoyed, and an inner bitterness began to rise in me against this creature whom nothing could disconcert and nothing could make suspicious.

"I wouldn't know," I answered roughly. "I wouldn't know anything about that. Let me tell you, moreover, once and for all that his name is Johan Arendt Happolati, judging from his initials."

"Johan Arendt Happolati," the man repeated, somewhat astonished at my violence. Then he fell silent.

"You should see his wife," I said, raving. "A fatter human being. . . . I suppose you don't think she was really fat?"

"Oh no, I certainly wouldn't deny that, especially—you know—that kind of a man . . ."

The old creature answered meekly and quietly to every one of my outbursts and fumbled for words as if he were afraid to say something wrong and make me angry.

"Goddammit, man, I suppose you think I've been sitting here stuffing you full of lies?" I shouted, completely out of my mind. "I'll bet you never believed there was a man with the name Happolati! Never in my life have I seen such obstinacy and viciousness in an old man! What in the hell has got hold of you anyway? And you have probably been thinking to yourself, on top of all this, that I am actually broke, haven't you, and that this is my best suit, and that I haven't a cigarette case in my

41

pocket at all? The way you have treated me is something I am not used to. I will tell you flatly, and I won't take it, so help me God, neither from you nor from anybody else, and you may as well know that now!"

The man got to his feet. He stood there with his mouth open, completely dumb, and listened to my outburst to the end; then he reached hurriedly for his bundle on the bench and walked away, nearly running down the path, with his little old man's steps.

I sat down on the bench and watched his back go farther and farther away, seeming to fold more and more in on itself. I don't know where the impression came from, but it occurred to me that I had never seen a more dishonest, a more vile back than this one, and I wasn't at all sorry that I had given him what he deserved before he left. . . .

The light began to fail, the sun was sinking, a faint rustling came from the trees nearby, and the nursemaids who were sitting in groups by the climbing bars got ready to push their baby carriages home. I was tranquil and in good spirits. The excited state I had just been in slowly passed away and I returned to normal, became relaxed, and began to feel sleepy. The huge amount of bread I had eaten was no longer bothering me particularly. I leaned back on the bench in a marvelous mood, closed my eyes, and became more and more drowsy; I slipped off and was about to fall into a deep sleep when a park attendant placed his hand on my shoulder and said, "You mustn't sleep sitting here."

"No, no," I said and jumped up. All at once the hideous position I was in drove in on me with all its force. I had to do something, light on something or other! Trying for a job had not worked; my recommendations were old by now and written by people so totally unknown they were virtually worthless anyway; and this series of refusals all through the summer had been a heavy blow to my morale. Nevertheless, my rent was due now, and I had to find a way out. Everything else would have to wait.

I had taken my pencil and paper out again and was sitting mechanically writing 1848 in all the corners. If only one good thought would rush in, then words would come! That had happened before, I had had times when I could write out a long piece with no effort at all, and it would turn out to be first-rate besides.

I wrote 1848 twenty times, wrote it crossways and intersecting and every possible way, waiting for a usable idea to come. A swarm of vague thoughts were batting about in my brain. The mood of the approaching dusk made me despondent and sentimental. Fall was here and had already begun to put everything into a deep sleep—the flies and small creatures had received their first shock; high in trees and down near the earth you could hear the sounds of a laboring life, breathing, restless, and rustling, struggling not to die. The whole community of insects would rouse themselves one more time, poke their yellow heads up out of the moss, lift their legs, put out expeditions, feeling with their long antennae, and then suddenly collapse, roll over, and turn their stomachs to the sky. Every plant had received the mark—the delicate breath of the first frost had passed over it. Grass stems held themselves stiffly up toward the sun, and the fallen leaves slipped across the ground with a sound like that of traveling silkworms. It was the hour of fall, well into the festival of what is not eternal. The roses have taken on a fever, their blood-red leaves have a strange and unnatural flush.

I myself felt like an insect about to go under, attacked by annihilation in this world ready to go to sleep. I jumped up, laboring with profound terrors, and took three or four long steps up the path. No! I cried, and clenched both fists, this has to end! And I sat down again, brought out the pencil and paper in order to grapple with the article. When the rent was right before my eyes, it would never do to give up.

My thoughts slowly started to assemble. I paid attention to them and wrote down with care a couple of well-thought-out pages, a sort of introduction: it could have been a beginning to several things, a travel piece or a political essay, whichever I felt like. The pages led one on, and made a good introduction to either sort of piece.

Next I started looking about for a specific question which I could discuss, a person, a problem I could fasten on. I couldn't come on anything. During this struggle, chaos began to appear again in my thoughts, I could feel my brain literally go click, my head began emptying, and finally it was balancing lightly and without content on my shoulders. I felt this ghastly emptiness inside with my whole body. I seemed to myself hollowed out from head to toe.

"Lord, my God and my Father!" I cried in agony, and I repeated this appeal many times in succession without adding a word.

The wind rustled in the leaves, it was getting ready to rain. I sat there a while yet and stared hopelessly at my papers, finally folded them together and placed them slowly in my pocket. The air had become chilly, and I had no waistcoat now; I turned my collar up to my neck, stuck my hands in my pockets, then stood up and left.

If it only could have gone this time, this one time! My landlady had inquired about the rent with her eyes twice now, and I had had to duck my head and sneak past with an embarrassed greeting. I could not do it again; the next time I met those eyes, I would release my room and make some honest nest for myself. The way it all was going, that time could not be far off.

When I came down to the park gate, I saw the little old troll again whom I had chased away in a rage. The mysterious bundle was lying alongside him on the bench, opened; in it were several sorts of food which he was just eating. I immediately had the impulse to go to him and apologize, ask him to forgive my behavior, but his food put me off. His ancient fingers, which looked like ten folded claws, were clutching the sandwiches in a repulsive way. I felt nauseated and walked past without speaking. He didn't recognize me; his eyes stared at me like dry horns and his face was entirely blank.

I walked on.

I stopped as I always did when I passed any newspaper building, and read the late editions posted outside in order to study the classified section for job openings, and this time I was lucky enough to find one I could apply for; a grocer on Grønland Street wanted someone for a few hours' bookkeeping every day; wages by arrangement. I wrote the man's address down and prayed to God silently for this position—I would accept much less than anybody else for the work, half a krone would be princely or perhaps even less; the price would not be a consideration.

When I got home I found on my table a note from my landlady in which she asked me either to pay my rent in advance or to move as soon as I could. I mustn't be offended at this, it was a request she had to make. With best wishes, Mrs. Gundersen.

I wrote a letter of application to the grocer, whose name was Christie, 31 Grønland Street, sealed the envelope and took it down to the mailbox at the corner. Then I went back up to my room and sat down to think in my rocking chair, as the room grew more and more dark. It was beginning to be difficult to stay up late now.

I woke very early the next morning. When I opened my eyes, it was still half dark, and it was quite a while before I heard the clock in the apartment beneath strike five. I wanted to fall asleep again, but couldn't manage it; I became more and more alert and lay there thinking thousands of things.

All at once, one or two remarkable sentences occurred to me, good for a short story or a sketch, windfalls in language, as good as I had ever come on. I lay saying the words over to myself and decided they were excellent. Soon several other sentences joined the two; instantly I was wide awake, stood up, and took paper and pencil from the table at the foot of my bed. It was like a vein opening, one word followed the other, arranged themselves in right order, created situations; scene piled on scene, actions and conversations welled up in my brain, and a strange sense of pleasure took hold of me. I wrote as if possessed, and filled one page after the other without a moment's pause. Thoughts poured in so abruptly, and kept on coming in such a stream, that I lost a number of them from not being able to write them down fast enough, even though I worked with all my energy. They continued to press themselves on me; I was deep into the subject, and every word I set down came from somewhere else.

The session lasted a wonderfully long time before it ended! I had fifteen, twenty written pages lying on my knees in front of me when I finally stopped and laid the pencil down. Now if those pages were only worth anything, I was saved! I leaped out of bed and dressed. It grew more and more light, and I could halfway make out the Chief of Lighthouses' message down by the door; near the window there was already enough light to write by, if one had to. I started immediately making a clean copy.

A strange mist, with lights and colors in it, rose from these fantasies; startled, I came on one good thing after the other and told myself that it was the best piece I had ever read in my life. I became giddy with contentment, gladness swelled up in me, I felt myself to be magnificent. I weighed the piece in my hand and assessed it on the spot with a rough guess as five kroner. No one would ever haggle about five kroner for this. On the contrary. In view of the quality, one could call it pure thievery to get the piece for ten. The last thing I had in mind was to do such a remarkable work free; my experience was that one did not find stories of that sort lying about on the street! I decided definitely on ten kroner.

It grew lighter and lighter in the room: I glanced down by the door and I could read without any great difficulty the delicate skeletonlike letters of Miss Andersen's offer of shrouds, Main Entrance, to the right; the clock had struck seven some time ago.

I stood up and remained standing in the center of the room. All in all, Mrs. Gundersen's notice had come rather conveniently. This really wasn't any room for me; the curtains on the windows were a very ordinary green, and there weren't even enough pegs on the walls to hang your wardrobe on. The sad rocking chair in the corner was actually a joke of a chair: if one started laughing at it, one could die laughing. It was too low for a grown man, and besides, it was so tight, one needed a shoehorn to get back out of it. In short, this room was simply not furnished in a way appropriate to intellectual effort, and I did not intend to keep it any longer. I would not keep it under any circumstances! I had been silent in this hole and stood it here and stayed on here too long already.

Borne up by hope and contentment, thinking all the time of my marvelous story, which I took out of my pocket every other minute to look at, I decided to get it over with right now and move. I took out my bundle, a red handkerchief which contained two clean collars and some crumpled newspaper which I had carried my bread home in, rolled it all together with my blanket, and added my store of white writing paper. Then, just to make sure, I looked in every corner to see that I hadn't left anything, and when nothing turned up, I walked to the window and looked out. The morning was dark and misty; no one had arrived yet at the burned-down smithy site and the clothes-line down in the courtyard was stretched tight from wall to wall, shrunken by the mist. There was nothing new, so I turned away from the window, took the blanket under my arm, bowed to the Chief of Lighthouses' announcement, bowed to Miss Andersen's shroud, and opened the door.

All at once I remembered the landlady; she certainly ought to be notified of my departure so she might realize that she was dealing with a self-respecting person. I wanted to thank her also in writing for the couple of days I had used the room beyond my time. The certainty that I was saved now for a long while dominated me so entirely that I even promised to give my landlady five kroner when I came into them one of these days: I wanted to prove to her without possibility of doubt what an honorable man she had had under her roof.

I left the note behind on the table.

I stopped by the door and turned around one more time. The delicious feeling of having come out on top at last filled me with joy and made me thankful to God and to the universe and I knelt down by the bed and thanked God aloud for His great goodness toward me that morn-

47

ıng. I knew, oh I knew so well, that the inspiration and holy breath I had just experienced and written down was a wonderful working of God in my soul, an answer to my cry of need of yesterday. It is God! It is God! I cried to myself, and I was so moved over my own words I sobbed; now and then I had to stop and listen a moment to hear if anyone should be coming up the stairs. At last I stood up and left; I slipped noiselessly down all the flights of stairs and made it to the outer door unseen.

The streets were shiny from the rain that had fallen in the dawn hours, the sky hung low and thick over the city, there was not a ray of sunlight anywhere. What would this day bring? I started as usual in the direction of the City Hall and saw that the clock showed eight-thirty. I had, therefore, a couple of hours to waste; there was no sense in getting to the newspaper office before ten, perhaps eleven; I could wander around till that time, and in the meantime think of some avenue that would lead to breakfast. The best was that I had no fear of going to bed hungry tonight; those times, thank God, were over! That phase was behind me now, a bad dream, from now on it was upward all the way!

But in the meantime my green blanket was becoming a problem; I certainly couldn't make a spectacle of myself carrying something like that around under my arm in broad daylight. What would people think of me? So I walked along trying to think of some place where it would be safe until later. It struck me suddenly that I could walk over to Semb's and have them wrap it. The bundle would instantly look more respectable and there would be no shame any longer in carrying it. I carried it into the store and communicated my errand to one of the clerks.

He looked first at the blanket, then at me; I had the sensation that he shrugged his shoulders, invisibly, with a kind of contempt, as he took the parcel. That wounded me.

"For God's sake, be careful!" I shouted. "Two delicate vases are inside. That package has to get to Smyrna!"

That helped immensely. With every movement of his

hands and body the clerk begged my forgiveness for not having sensed that there were expensive objects inside the blanket. When he had finished his wrapping, I thanked him for his help like a man who has often sent valuable objects to Smyrna. He even opened the door for me as I left.

I started wandering around among the people in the main marketplace, and particularly hovered near the women who were selling potted plants. The heavy red roses smoldering in the foggy morning, blood-colored and uninhibited, made me greedy, and tempted me powerfully to steal one—I asked the prices merely so I could come as near them as possible. If I got more money than I needed, I would buy one, no matter what happened afterwards; I could always skimp a little here and there in my daily budget to make up for it.

It was ten, and I walked to the newspaper office. Scissors, who spent his day cutting out news notes from other newspapers, was absently leafing through old issues, the editor had not yet come in. Following Scissors' inquiry, I delivered over my great manuscript to him, made him understand that it was a matter of more than ordinary importance, and impressed firmly on his mind that the editor should receive it personally as soon as he arrived. I would pop in later in the day for his answer myself.

"Very good!" Scissors said, and went back to his paper.

It seemed to me he had taken it a little too calmly, but I said nothing, just nodded casually to him and left.

Now I had a lot of time. If the weather would only clear up! It was really a miserable day, nothing fresh, no wind; the women were using umbrellas just to be safe, and the wool hats of the men looked comical. I made one more trip through the market to see the vegetables and the roses. I felt a hand on my shoulder, and turned: "Queeny" was saying good morning.

"Good morning, yes," I answered in a questioning tone in order to find out what he wanted as quickly as possible. I was not too fond of Queeny.

He looked curiously at the brand-new package under my arm and asked, "What have you there?"

"I bought some cloth at Semb's for a suit," I answered in a casual tone. "I don't know why I should go around so threadbare any longer; one can be too stingy in bodily things too, you know."

He looked at me intently.

"How is it going then?" he said slowly.

"Fine, much better than I had expected."

"Have you found something to do then?"

"Something to do?" I answered and looked mightily surprised. "I am the bookkeeper at the Christie Foodstore."

"Is that so?" he said, and drew back a little. "You have no idea how happy I am about that. Just so friends don't get it all away from you. Goodbye."

A few seconds later, he turned around and came back. He pointed with his stick to my parcel and said, "Let me recommend my tailor for your suit. You'll never, never find a better tailor than Isaksen. Just say I sent you."

Why was he sticking his nose into my business? What was it to him which tailor I used? I got angry. The sight of this aimless, painted-up creature somehow enraged me and I reminded him in a brutal tone of the ten kroner he had borrowed from me. Before he had even replied, I regretted having asked him for it; I felt ashamed and didn't look him in the eyes. At that moment a woman came along, I stepped quickly back to let her go by, and then took the opportunity to slip away.

What should I do with myself, waiting? I couldn't sit in a café with an empty pocketbook, and I couldn't think of any acquaintances I could go visit at this time of day. I headed instinctively for the upper part of town, got rid of some time on the way between the marketplace and Grænsen Street, read the *Afternoon Times* which had just been posted outside the office, made a swing down Karl Johan, turned around again, and walked straight to Our Saviour's Church yard, where I found a quiet bench on the slope near the chapel. I sat there in privacy, dozing in the damp air, and daydreamed, half asleep and chilly. Time passed. Was it absolutely certain that my sketch was a small masterpiece and inspired?

God knows it wasn't free of faults here and there! Everything considered, it could very well not be accepted, no, simply not accepted! Maybe it was not entirely free of mediocrity, maybe it was downright bad—how did I know but that at this very moment it wasn't already in the wastebasket? My peace of mind was shaken; I leaped up and rushed out of the cemetery.

Once on Akers Street again, I glanced into a shop window and saw that it was only a few minutes past twelve. This made me despair even more. I had been so sure it was long past noon; there was no sense in visiting the editor before four. I had ominous feelings about the fate of my sketch; the more I thought about it, the more unreasonable it seemed that I could have written anything worthwhile in such a short time, and half asleep besides, and my brain wild and feverish. I had deceived myself, that's all, had been overjoyed all morning for nothing! That's all! . . . I walked with long steps up Ullevaals Street, past the St. Hanshaugen district, came to the edge of town, walked through building sites and farmers' fields and finally found myself on a country road that went on farther than I could see.

I stopped there and decided to turn around. The walk had made me warm, and I walked back slowly and extremely depressed. I met two hayracks, the drivers lying on their backs on top of the loads, singing. Both were bareheaded, with round faces untouched by grief. I thought to myself as I walked along that they were sure to say something, throw out some remark or other, play a practical joke. When I was near enough, one of them shouted, asking me what I had under my arm.

"A blanket," I answered.

"What time is it?" he asked.

"I'm not sure, about three I think."

The two laughed and drove by. As they did, I felt the flick of a whip on one ear and my hat was jerked off. They couldn't let me get by without some sort of prank. Furiously, I reached for my ear, picked my hat up from the ditch, and went on. Farther on, in St. Hanshaugen, I met a man who informed me that it was already past four.

Past four! It was already past four! I pulled up stakes for town and the newspaper office. Perhaps the editor had already been there and left! I walked and ran around everyone, stumbled, bumped against wagons, left all the other pedestrians behind, ran even with the horses, hurried like a madman to get there in time. I twisted in through the outer door, took the stairs in four leaps, and knocked.

No one answered.

He's gone! He's gone! I thought. I tried the door. It was open. I knocked once more and walked in.

The editor was sitting at his desk, his face turned to the window, his pen in hand about to write. When he heard my panting good day, he turned halfway around, glanced at me, shook his head, and said: "I haven't had time yet to read your piece."

I was so overjoyed that he hadn't tossed it out yet that I said, "No, I understand that. There's no hurry about it. A couple of days, maybe, or . . . ?"

"Well, we'll see. In any event, I have your address."

And I forgot to tell him that I no longer had an address.

The audience was over; I stepped back, bowing, and left. Hope blazed up in me again, nothing was lost yet, on the contrary, I could still win, be utterly victorious, for that matter. And my brain instantly fell to imagining a great council in heaven where it had just this moment been decided that I should win, receive ten kroner flat for my story. . . .

If I only had somewhere to stay tonight! I debated the best place to poke myself into, and was so absorbed in this question that I stopped still in the center of the street. I forgot where I was and stood like a solitary buoy in the middle of the ocean with the water flowing and roaring around it. A paperboy held out the evening paper *Viking* to me. "Get it here, sensational!" I looked up and started—I was outside Semb's again.

I quickly turned my back, hid the parcel in front of me, and hurried down Kirke Street worried and ashamed that they might have noticed me from the window. I passed Ingebret's and the theater, and at the ticket office turned down toward the harbor and the fortress. I found another bench and started casting about again.

How in God's name would I find a room tonight? Maybe there was a hole somewhere I could slip into and stay hidden in until morning? My pride would not allow me to go back to the room I had: nothing could ever force me to go back on my word. I pushed that thought away with great indignation and smiled arrogantly to myself about the tiny red rocking chair. By an association of ideas, I suddenly found myself in a large, two-windowed room I had once had on Hægdehaugen Street, I saw a tray on the table full of thick slices of bread and butter. It shifted its features, now it was a piece of beef, a tempting piece, a snow-white napkin, all sorts of bread, a silver fork. The door opened: my landlady came in offering me more tea. . . .

Delusions and dreams! I told myself that if I did eat food now, my head would get upset again, I would have the same feverish brain and ridiculous ideas to deal with. I simply couldn't take food, I wasn't made that way; that was one of my characteristics, a peculiar thing with me.

Perhaps some possibility of a bed would turn up when it was nearer evening. There was no hurry; at the worst, I could always find a place out in the woods; the entire environs of the city were at my disposal and the weather could not be regarded as cold yet.

In front of me, the sea rocked in its heavy drowsiness; ships and fat, broad-nosed barges dug up graves in the lead-colored plain, shiny waves darted out the right and left and kept going, and all the time the smoke poured like feathery quilts out of the smokestacks and the sound of pistons penetrated faintly through the heavy moist air. There was no sun and no wind, the trees behind me were wet, and the bench I sat on was cold and damp. Time passed; I settled down to doze a little; grew sleepy and a bit chilly in my back. Soon after, I felt my eyes begin to close. I let them close . . .

When I woke, it was all dark around me, I jumped up confused and half frozen, grabbed my parcel and started walking. I walked faster and faster to warm up, beat my arms, rubbed my lower legs, which were numb, and came up near the firehouse. It was nine; I had slept several hours.

What should I do now? I had to go somewhere. I stood gaping up at the firehouse, wondering if it would be possible to slip in one of the entrances and go through just the instant when the guard's back was turned. I climbed the stairs intending to engage the guard in conversation; he immediately lifted his ax in present-arms position, waiting to see what I had to say. This ax, lifted with its edge toward me, was like a cold blow right through my nerves: I became mute with fright before this armed man and involuntarily started to retreat. I didn't say a word, just slipped steadily backward. To save face, I rubbed my hand over my forehead as if I had forgotten something, and sneaked off. When I was standing on the sidewalk again, I felt saved, as if I had just escaped from a tremendous danger. I hurried away.

Cold and hungry, more and more miserable, I pushed on down Karl Johan Street. I started to swear, not caring whether anyone could hear me or not. Near the Senate House, just where the trees begin, a new association of ideas called up a painter I knew, a young man whom I had once saved from a brawl in the amusement park, and whom I later had visited. I snapped my fingers and took off down Tordenskjold Street, found a door with a card on it reading C. Zacharias Bartel, and knocked.

He came to the door himself; he gave off a ghastly reek of beer and tobacco.

"Good evening!" I said.

"Good evening! Is it you? Why in hell have you come so late? It can't be seen really in artificial light. I've added a hayrack since you saw it last, and changed a few things. You must see it in the daylight, there's no use looking at it now."

"Let me see it now anyway!" I said. Actually, I couldn't think what painting he was standing there talking about.

"Absolutely, totally impossible!" he answered. "The whole thing would look yellow! Also, there's one more thing." He leaned toward me, whispering, "I have a little girl visitor tonight, so we'll have to give it up."

"Oh, yes, well, yes, you're right, there's no question then."

I stepped down, said good night, and left.

So there was no way out of it then but to find some place out in the woods. If only the ground hadn't been so damp! I patted my blanket and felt more and more relieved at the thought of sleeping out. I had spent so much time looking for a room in the city that I was sick and tired of the whole thing. I felt a delicious pleasure in letting it all go, just relaxing and floating along the street without a worry in my head. I walked to the clock at the university, saw that it was after ten, and from there I headed north. I stopped once on Hægdehaugen Street outside a grocery store that had some food displayed in the window. A cat lay there asleep beside a French loaf, just behind it was a bowl of lard and several jars of meal. I stood for a while looking at these groceries, but since I had nothing to buy them with, I turned away and pushed on. I walked very slowly, finally passed Majorstuen, walked on and on, walked for hours, and at last got out to the Bogstad Woods.

I left the road here and sat down to rest. Then I started looking for a likely place, gathered together some ling and juniper boughs and made a bed on top of a little hill where it was moderately dry. I opened my parcel and took out the blanket. I was exhausted from the long walk and lay down immediately. I tried all sorts of positions before I finally got settled down: my ear smarted somewhat, it was slightly swollen from the crack the farm worker had given it and I couldn't lie on it. I took off my shoes and put them under my head with the wrapping paper on top of them.

The darkness brooded around me. Nothing moved. But high above my head rustled endless music, the air, that distant tuneless humming which never fell silent. I listened so long to this eternal feeble sound that it began to get me confused: it was certainly symphonies coming from the orbiting universes above me, stars that were singing a song. . . .

"It's not, more likely the devil!" I said, and laughed aloud to bolster me a little. "It is the night owls of Canaan hooting!"

I got up, lay down again, put on my shoes, tramped around awhile in the dark, and lay down again, fought and battled against rage and terror till far into the morning hours, when I finally fell asleep.

It was broad daylight when I woke, and I had the feeling it was near noon. I put on my shoes, wrapped up my blanket, and started back to town. No sun today either, and I was shivering like a dog. My feet were numb and water began to come out of my eyes as though they couldn't bear the light.

It was three in the afternoon. My hunger began to be painful. I was weak, and walked along throwing up here and there on the sly. I took a swing down to the Steam Kitchen, read the menu and twitched my shoulders in case anyone was watching, as though to say corned meat and pork were not food for me; after that, I walked down by the railroad station.

All at once a curious confusion slipped into my head; I walked on, not wanting to pay any attention to it, but it grew worse and worse; finally I had to sit down on a doorstep. My whole consciousness underwent some change, a tissue in my brain parted. I took a couple of breaths and remained sitting there astonished. I was conscious, I could feel clearly a little pain in my ear from yesterday, and when an acquaintance came by, I knew him immediately and stood up to give him a small nod and bow.

What sort of a new and painful sensation was this, which was being added to the others? Did it come from sleeping on the ground? Or was it because I hadn't had breakfast yet? All in all, there was absolutely no sense in living in this way; and by Holy Christ I did not understand what I had done to deserve this clear persecution either! Suddenly it struck me that I could just as well make a rat of myself right now and take the blanket off to "Uncle's" artesian well. I could pawn it for a krone and get three respectable meals, and keep myself going until I found something else—I would have to get around Hans Pauli later. I was already on my way to the well when I stopped in front of the entrance, shook my head doubtfully, and then turned around.

After I was some distance away, I grew more and more glad that I had won this severe test. The awareness that I was honorable rose to my head, filled me with magnificent conviction that I had character. I was a white beacon tower in the middle of a dirty human ocean full of floating wreckage. To pawn someone else's property for a single meal, to eat and drink oneself into damnation, to look in your own face and call yourself rat and have to drop your eyes—never! Never! I had never really seriously considered it; it had just occurred to me loosely; a man wasn't really responsible for these accidental, floating notions, especially when he had a ghastly headache and had nearly killed himself dragging around a blanket that belonged to another person.

There will certainly be some way to find help in any case when the time comes! For example, the grocer on Grønland Street, had I been pestering him every hour on the hour since I answered his ad? Had I rung his bell too early and too late and been sent away? I hadn't so much as appeared there once for my answer! The effort might not be entirely in vain—maybe luck was with me this time. Luck had a habit of following curious paths. So I went off to Grønland Street.

The last disturbance that had swept through my brain had left me a bit faint, and I walked very slowly, thinking about what I would say to the grocer. He could very well be a good soul. If the whim struck him, he might give me a krone in advance, even, without my asking for it: people like that now and then get wonderful notions in their heads.

I slipped into a doorway and darkened my trouser knees with a little spit so I'd look respectable, stowed my

57

blanket behind a box in one dark corner, strode across the street, and entered the small store.

A man was standing there pasting bags together from old newspapers.

I said that I would like to speak with Mr. Christie.

"That is me," the man answered.

So! My name was such and so, I had taken the liberty of answering his advertisement, and I was wondering if he had been able to use me.

He repeated my name several times and began to laugh. "Well, we'll see now!" he said, and took my letter out of his pocket. "Would you be so good as to note how you deal with figures, my good man? You have dated this letter with the year 1848." And he laughed from deep in his chest.

"Yes, that was a shame," I said, crestfallen, "a moment of absent-mindedness, distraction, I admit it."

"Well, you see I have to have a man who doesn't make mistakes with figures," he said. "I regret it—your handwriting is extremely clear, I liked your letter also, but . . ."

I waited a little while; it was inconceivable that was the man's last word. He went back to making his paper bags.

"Yes, that's embarrassing," I said. "A gruesome embarrassment, but of course it won't happen again, and this slip of the pen surely can't have made me totally unfit to keep books?"

"No, I didn't say that," he answered, "but for the moment it seemed important enough to me so that I decided on another man on the spot."

"So the position is taken then?" I asked.

"Yes."

"Good Lord, then there's nothing more to do about it!"

"No. I'm sorry about it, but . . ."

"Goodbye!" I said.

Now a brutal rage blazed up in me. I took my parcel from the entry, ground my teeth, ran into peaceful pedestrians on the sidewalks and did not ask pardon. When one man stopped and scolded me in a sharp tone for my behavior, I turned around, screamed a solitary meaningless word into his ear, and shook my fist right under his nose. I walked on, frightened by a blind rage I could not control. He called to a policeman. I wanted nothing more at that moment than to have a policeman between my two hands for a minute, so I slowed my pace on purpose to give him time to catch me, but no one came. Was there some particular reason why absolutely every last one of a man's most serious and most sincere endeavors should fail? Why had I written 1848 anyway? What was that damned year to me? Now I was walking around starving so that my intestines were curling up inside me like snakes, and moreover there was no guarantee that food would come to me by the day's end either. And as time went on, I was becoming spiritually and physically more and more hollowed out, I let myself sink to less and less honorable deeds every day. I told blank lies without a blush, cheated poor people out of their rent, and fought against the grossest impulses to make off with someone else's blanket, all without remorse, without bad conscience. Rotten patches were beginning to appear in my insides, black spongy areas that were spreading. And up in heaven God was sitting, keeping an open eye on me, and taking care that my defeat proceed after the correct rules of the art, evenly and slowly, with no break in rhythm. But in the pit of hell the evil devils roamed around bursting with rage because it was taking me so long to commit a mortal sin, an unforgivable sin, one for which God in His righteousness would have to throw me down. . . .

I increased my pace, pushed myself faster and faster, swung suddenly to the left, and strode excitedly and angrily into a light, elegant entry. I did not stop, did not pause a second—yet my consciousness took in the whole decorative arrangement of the vestibule in that half second: every insignificant detail of the doors, molding, floor tiling was utterly clear to me inwardly as I sprang up the stairs. I rang a bell violently on the third floor. Why did I stop precisely on the third floor? And why did I choose this bell, which was farthest from the stair?

A young woman in a gray dress, trimmed with black, opened the door. She looked at me astonished for a little while, then shook her head and said, "No, we don't have anything for you today." And she made a motion to close the door.

Why had I thrown myself in the path of this person? She took me obviously to be a beggar; suddenly I became cool and calm. I took off my hat and made a proper bow; then as if I had not heard her sentence, I said in the politest conceivable voice, "I do beg your pardon, madam, for having rung so loud. I wasn't familiar with your bell. I believe that there is an invalid gentleman here who has advertised for a man to give him outings in a chair?"

She stood still awhile, trying out this fantastic lie on her tongue; she seemed to be undecided about me.

"No," she said finally, "there is no invalid gentleman here."

"Are you sure? An elderly man, two hours' outing each day, half krone an hour?"

"No."

"Then I must ask you for your pardon again," I said. "Possibly it is the second floor. In any case, I merely wanted to recommend for the post a man in whom I have taken an interest. My own family is Wedel-Jarlsberg." Then I bowed once more and withdrew. The young woman turned beet red and in her embarrassment could not move from the spot but stood rooted staring after me as I went down the stairs.

My peace of mind was back, and my brain clear. The woman's words saying she had nothing to give me today had affected me like a cold shower of rain. It had gone so far now that everybody in the world could glance at me and say to himself: There goes a beggar, one of those people who get their food handed to them through a door!

On Møller Street I stopped outside a restaurant and sniffed the marvelous odor of meat cooking inside; I had already put my hand on the doorknob and was ready to drift in when I caught myself in time and walked away. When I got down to the main market square, I looked around for a place to sit but found all the benches taken. I walked around the church on all sides looking for a quiet place to flop down. Naturally! I said bitterly to myself, naturally, what else! I started to walk again. I made a swing past the corner fountain and took a swallow of water, started to walk once more, dragged myself along, one foot after the other, stopped a long while outside every store window, turned to watch every wagon as it rattled past. I felt a sort of shimmering heat inside my head, and the beating in my temples was strange. The water I had drunk did not agree with me, and I walked on, throwing up a little here, a little there, in the gutter. Finally I made it to the Cemetery of Christ. I sat down with my elbows on my knees, my head in my hands: bent over like that, it was better, and I didn't feel the small gnawing in my chest any longer.

A stonecutter was lying on his stomach on top of a huge granite slab nearby, cutting an inscription; he was wearing blue spectacles and reminded me suddenly of an acquaintance whom I had nearly forgotten, a man who worked in a bank; I had met him some time ago in the Oplandske Café.

If I could just get rid of shame once and for all and go to him! Tell him the truth right out, that the situation was becoming desperate for me now, it was getting difficult to stay alive! I could give him my barber coupons. . . . Holy God, my barber coupons! coupons worth up to a krone! I rummaged anxiously for this valuable treasure. When I didn't find it fast enough, I leaped up, searched, sweating with fear, and found them at last at the bottom of my breast pocket, along with other papers, some blank, some written on, all of no value. I counted the six coupons many times forward and backward. I didn't have much use for them—it might be taken as a whim of mine, an eccentricity, that I no longer bothered to shave. I had help to the value of half a krone, a good silver half krone from the Kongsberg mine! The banks closed at six, I could probably find my man at the Oplandske Café around seven or eight.

I sat up and warmed myself for a long time with this

thought. Time went by, the chestnut leaves around me moved heavily in the wind, the day was ending. Wasn't it really a little sordid to come sneaking up with six barber coupons to a gentleman who occupied a post in a bank? Maybe he had two barber books in marvelous shape in his pocket, coupons entirely different from mine, clean and crisp ones, very likely. I felt in all my pockets for a couple of things I could give him to boot, but found nothing. Suppose I offered him my tie? I could easily spare that now as long as I just buttoned my coat a little tighter, and I had to do that anyway since I no longer had a waistcoat. I took my tie off—it was the large formal kind and covered half my chest—brushed it off carefully, and wrapped it in a piece of white writing paper together with my barber coupons. Then I left the churchyard and started for the café.

The clock on the city jail said seven. I hovered about the café, poked about along the iron fence, and kept an eye on everyone going in or out. Finally, at about eight I saw him coming, fresh and elegantly dressed, up the hill; he cut across the street toward the café. My heart beat wildly like a little bird in my chest as I caught sight of him, and without even saying hello, I blurted out something.

"A half krone, my friend!" I said, becoming impertinent. "Here—here is fair exchange for it!" and I pushed the little packet into his hand.

"Don't have it!" he said. "Swear to God!" And he turned his coin purse inside out for me. "I was out last night, and I'm broke; believe me, it's absolutely true."

"No, no, I believe you, old boy!" I said and took him at his word. There was in fact no reason for him to lie with so little at stake; it struck me, too, that his blue eyes were a bit moist as he rummaged in his pocket, finding nothing. I took a step back.

"Forgive the whole thing!" I said. "I wasn't in a really big fix anyway."

I was already half a block down the street when he called after me about the packet.

"Keep it, keep it!" I answered. "You are very welcome

to it! It is only a couple of small things, doesn't amount to anything—about everything I own in the world." I was moved by my own words, which sounded so pathetic in the early twilight, and I started to cry.

The wind sprang up, the clouds hurried across the sky, and it became cooler and cooler as it got dark. I walked along crying down the entire street to its end, feeling more and more pity for myself, and I repeated again and again several words, a cry from the heart which would always start the tears once more when they were about to stop: "My God and my Lord, I have such tribulation!"

An hour went by in this way, endlessly, slowly, sluggishly. I puttered about on Torv Street for a long time, sat on steps, slipped into doorways when anyone came by, or stood staring blankly into the shops where people were bustling around with merchandise and money; finally I found myself a cozy place behind a pile of lumber between the church and the market tents.

Well, I definitely could not go back to the woods tonight, no matter what happened, I didn't have energy enough for it, it was too far out there. I would get through the night as best I could, where I was—if it got too cold I could always walk a few times around the church. I didn't need to make any elaborate plans for that. So I leaned back and dozed.

The noise around me grew less, the shops were closed. I heard fewer and fewer steps of passers-by; finally all the windows around me were dark. . . .

I opened my eyes and became aware of a shape standing in front of me; the shiny buttons that glittered in my direction made me guess a policeman. I couldn't see the man's face.

"Good evening!" he said.

"Good evening!" I answered, and felt afraid. I stood up somewhat embarrassed. He stood awhile without moving.

"Do you live near here?" he asked.

Without thinking, out of sheer habit, I named my old address, the little attic room I had left.

He stood quiet a moment.

"Have I done anything wrong?" I asked in anxiety.

"Oh no, not at all!" he answered. "But I think it is time for you to go home now, it's cold lying here."

"Yes, it is chilly, I can feel it."

So I said good night and instinctively made my way to my old place. Now if I were only careful I could go up without being heard—there were eight flights of stairs in all, and only the two top ones had creaky steps.

I took my shoes off downstairs and started up. The house was quiet. On the third floor I heard the slow tick-tock of a clock, and a child who cried a little; after that, I heard nothing. I found my door, lifted it a bit on its hinges and opened it without using the key, as I often did; I walked in and closed the door silently behind me.

Everything was just as I had left it—the curtains were pulled aside, and the bed was empty. On the table I caught a glint from some paper, probably my note to the land-lady. The chances were she hadn't even been up here then since I had left. I ran my hands over the white spot and found to my surprise that it was a letter. A letter? I took it over to the window and studied as well as I could in the dark the scrawl of the address, and at last made out my own name. Aha! I thought, the landlady's reply, warning me not to set foot in the room again, if I had such an idea!

Then I walked slowly, very slowly, out of the room, carrying my shoes in one hand and the letter in the other, my blanket under my arm. I tiptoed and grit my teeth on the creaking steps and made it safely down all the stairs and finally stood in the entryway once more.

I put my shoes on again, taking a good long time ty-ing the laces, sat for a moment motionless when I was done, stared blankly ahead of me, holding the letter in my hands.

Then I stood up and walked away.

A gas lamp was flickering up the street, so I walked right under it, rested my parcel against the lamppost, and opened the letter, doing it all with an exaggerated slow-ness.

The letter shot through me like a stream of light, and

I heard myself give a little cry, a meaningless sound of joy: the letter was from the editor, my piece was accepted, being set in type immediately! "A few minor changes . . . a couple of typographical errors corrected . . . shows real ability . . . will appear tomorrow . . . ten kroner."

I laughed and cried, leaped in the air and ran down the street, stopped and beat my legs, swore wholesale at no one about nothing. And time went by.

The whole night until dawn I went yodeling around the streets, dumfounded with joy, and said over and over: shows real ability, actually a little masterpiece, a stroke of genius. And ten kroner!

PART TWO

A COUPLE of weeks later I found myself out of doors one night. I had been sitting in one of the cemeteries again, working on an article for a newspaper; while I was still writing, it got to be 10 p.m., the darkness came, and the gate was about to be locked. I was hungry, terrifically hungry; the ten kroner had unfortunately not gone very far. Now it was two, nearly three, days since I had eaten anything and I felt faint—moving the pencil was almost too much effort. I had the blade part of a pocketknife and a bunch of keys in my pocket, but not a trace of money.

After the cemetery gate was locked, I should have gone straight home, but I felt an instinctive dread of my dark and empty room—an abandoned tinsmith's workshop I had finally gotten permission to stay in for the time being. So I staggered instead on down the street, roamed aimlessly past the city jail, all the way to the harbor and to a bench on the railroad pier, where I sat down.

For a few moments I didn't have a single sad thought. I forgot my troubles and felt peaceful looking at the harbor that lay serene and lovely in the dusk. I had the habit of cheering myself up by reading through the article I had just written, which always seemed to my afflicted brain the very best piece I had done. I pulled my manuscript out of my pocket, held it close up to my eyes, and read through one page after the other. Finally I grew tired and put the papers in my pocket. Everything was still; the sea stretched away like bluish mother-of-pearl, and small birds flew silently past me, going from one place to another. A policeman walked up and down a little way off. Otherwise, not a person could be seen, and the entire harbor was silent.

I counted up my money once more: one half a pocket-knife, one key chain, but not an øre. Suddenly I reached into my pocket and pulled the papers up once more. It was an automatic thing to do, an unconscious reflex. I found a white page among them, not written on, and— God knows where I got the idea—I folded it into a cone and closed it carefully so that it looked as though it was full, and then threw it as far as I could out in front of me. The wind carried it a little farther, then it lay there quietly.

Hunger was beginning to attack me now. I sat staring at the white paper cornucopia, which looked as though swollen by shiny silver coins, and I egged myself on to believe that it really did contain something. I sat there inviting myself in a normal voice to guess how much was in it—if I guessed right, the money was mine! I imagined the small exquisite ten-øre coins at the bottom and the fat, fluted krone pieces on top—a whole paper cone full of money! I sat gazing at it with huge eyes and urged myself to go and steal it.

Then I heard the policeman cough—and why did it suddenly occur to me to do the same? I stood up and coughed, repeating the cough three times so he would be sure to hear it. Now, won't he jump for that paper cone when he comes near? I sat rejoicing over this joke, I rubbed my hands in ecstasy and swore magnificently. His nose will stretch when he sees that! After this trick, he'll want to sink into the hottest puddle in hell! I had become intoxicated with starvation, my hunger had made me drunk.

A few minutes later the policeman came along, clicking his iron heels on the stones, keeping watch to all sides. He took his time, he had the whole night before him: he didn't see the paper cone until it was very close. Then he stopped and stared at it. It looked so white and valuable lying there, perhaps a little purse of money, no? A little store of silver? . . . He picked it up. Hmmm! It is light, very light. Maybe an expensive feather, decoration for a hat. . . . He opened it carefully with his large hands and peeked in. I laughed, I laughed and hit my knees, I laughed like a madman. And not a sound came from my mouth, my laughter was feverish and silent, it was intense like a sob. . . .

Then the stones clattered again, and the policeman made a swing back over the pier. I sat there with tears in my eyes, hiccuping from shortness of breath, out of my mind with feverish laughter. I started to talk aloud, told myself the story of the paper cone, mimicked the gestures of the poor policeman, peeked into my empty hand, and repeated again and again: He coughed when he threw it away! He coughed when he threw it away! I joined new phrases to these sentences, made titillating additions, revised the whole story, and brought it to the point: he coughed only once—haugh, haugh!

I exhausted all my variations on these words and it was well on into the evening before my gaiety subsided. A sleepy calm came over me, a lovely fatigue which I couldn't oppose. The darkness was thicker now, a light breeze furrowed the pearl-gray sea. The ships whose masts I could see outlined against the sky looked, with their black bodies, like silent monsters who had raised their bristles and were laying in wait for me. I had no pain, the hunger had smoothed that out. Instead I felt pleasantly empty, untouched by anything around me, glad to be unseen by everybody. I put my legs up on the bench and leaned back—in that position I could feel best the good feeling of isolation. There wasn't a cloud in my mind, not a suggestion of discomfort; I had not a single desire or longing unfulfilled so far as my thoughts could reach. I lay with eyes open in a sense of alienation from myself. I felt wonderfully out of myself.

Not a sound came to disturb me—the soft dark had hidden the whole world from me, and buried me in a wonderful peace—only the desolate voice of stillness sounded monotonously in my ear. And the dark monsters out there wanted to pull me to themselves as soon as night came, and they wanted to take me far far over seas and through strange lands where no human being lives. And they wanted to bring me to Princess Ylayali's castle, where an undreamed-of happiness was waiting for me, greater than any person's! And she herself would be sitting in a blazing room all of whose walls were amethyst, on a throne of yellow roses, and she would reach her hands out to me when I entered, greet me, and cry "Welcome" as I came near to her and kneeled: "Welcome, O knight, to me and to my land! I have been waiting twenty summers for you, and have called your name every bright summer night, and when you were in grief I wept here, and when you slept I breathed marvelous dreams into your head. . . ." And the beautiful creature took my hand as I rose, and led me on through long corridors where huge crowds of people shouted Hurrah, through sunlit orchards where three hundred young girls were playing and laughing, and into another chamber made all of brilliant emerald. The sun shone into it, choral music floated through galleries and halls toward me, perfumed air moved over me. I held her hand in mine, and felt a mad occult delight shoot through my blood; I put my arms around her and she whispered: "Not here, come farther in!" So we walked into the red chamber all of whose walls were ruby—an overwhelming joy which made me faint. Then I felt her arms around me, she breathed in my face, whispering: "Welcome now, my sweet! Kiss me! Again . . . again. . . ."

From my bench I saw stars in front of my eyes and my thought shot forward into a tornado of light. . . .

I had fallen asleep where I lay, and the policeman was waking me. I sat up, ruthlessly called back to life and misery. My first sensation was a stupid astonishment at finding myself out in the open air, but soon a bitter depression replaced that; I was just on the point of crying with grief over still being alive. It had been raining while I slept, my clothes were soaked through, and I felt a damp chill in my legs. The darkness was thicker, and it took effort to make out clearly the policeman's face in front of me.

"That's right," he said. "Stand up now!"

I stood up instantly: if he had ordered me to lie down again, I would have obeyed also. I felt hopeless and without energy; on top of that, I began almost immediately to feel the hunger again.

"Wait a minute, you idiot," the policeman cried after me. "You're leaving your hat behind! O.K., now go ahead!"

"I knew there was something I—something I'd forgotten," I stammered in true absent-mindedness. "Thanks. Good night."

And I staggered off.

If a man only had a bite to eat! Bread—one of those marvelous loaves of rye bread that a man could chew on as he walked. I walked along, deciding on exactly the kind of rye bread that would be best now. I was unbelievably hungry, longed to be dead and gone, became sentimental and cried. My road of misery would never end! All of a sudden I stopped on the street, stamped on the cobblestones, and swore aloud. What was it he had called me? Idiot? I would show that policeman what it meant to call me an idiot. Then I turned around and ran back down the street. I felt fiery hot with anger. Toward the bottom of the street I stumbled and fell, but hardly noticed it, jumped up again and ran on. By the time I got to the railway station I was so tired that I didn't feel able to keep on all the way to the pier; besides, during the run my anger had subsided. I stopped for breath. What was the difference what a policeman said?—"Yes, but there are some things I won't stand for!" "You're right!" I interrupted myself. "But he didn't know any better!" This excuse calmed me down; I repeated to myself that he didn't know any better. So I turned around a second time.

My God, what weird things you get into! I said angrily to myself—running like a madman on wet streets when it is black as pitch! The pains of hunger were unbearable and never let me alone. I swallowed spit over and over to take the edge off, and I felt it did some good. I had had very little to eat generally for several weeks, even before this current trouble, and my strength now was falling off noticeably. Whenever I had been lucky and scraped up five kroner by some maneuver or other, the money never managed to last long enough to get me back on my feet before a new famine fell on me. My back and my shoulders bothered me most; the small ache in my chest I could stop for a moment by coughing hard or walking carefully bent over, but my back and shoulders I couldn't do anything with. How could it be that nothing ever turned up for me! Didn't I have the same right to life as anybody else, Pascha, the rare-book seller, for example, or Hennechen, the steamship clerk? And didn't I have shoulders like a giant and two strong arms for work, and hadn't I in fact tried to get a job chopping wood on Møller Street to earn my bread? Was I lazy? Hadn't I applied for jobs, and listened to lectures, and written articles, and read and worked night and day like a madman? And hadn't I lived like a miser, eaten bread and milk when I was rich, bread when I wasn't, and gone hungry when I had nothing? Did I live in a hotel, did I have a suite of rooms on the second floor? I lived in a shack, a loft, in a tinsmith's shop deserted by both God and man since last winter because snow came in. So I had nothing at all to rebuke myself with on that score.

I walked along thinking all this over, and there wasn't even so much as a spark of malice or envy or bitterness in my brain.

Outside a paint store I stopped and looked in the window; I tried to read the labels on a couple of cans, but it was too dark. Angry at myself for this new whim, and upset and irritated that I couldn't find out what the labels said, I banged once on the window and then went on. Farther along I saw a police officer, speeded up, sidled up to him, and without the slightest preamble said, "It's ten o'clock."

"No, it's two," he answered, surprised.

"No, it's ten," I said. "It's ten o'clock." Growling with

anger, I went two steps nearer, clenched my fist, and said, "Listen, take my word for it, it's ten o'clock."

He stood meditating this for a bit, looking me over and gazing at me, baffled. Finally he said very softly, "In any case, it's certainly time for you to be going home. Would you like me to walk with you partway?"

This gesture of friendliness disarmed me. I felt tears coming to my eyes, and I quickly said, "No, thank you! I have just been out at a club a little too late. I'm much obliged to you."

He raised his hand and touched his hat as I left. His friendliness had overwhelmed me and I cried because I didn't have a five-kroner piece to give him. I stood looking after him as he slowly wandered on, hit myself on the forehead, and the farther he got away, the louder I sobbed. I cursed myself for my poverty, called myself various names, discovered wounding phrases for myself, priceless and rich finds of abusive terms which I heaped on myself. I kept this up until I was nearly home. When I got to the door, I discovered I had lost my keys.

Yes, naturally, I said bitterly to myself, why not indeed, why shouldn't I have lost them? Here I have my home, in a place that is a stable downstairs and a tinsmith shop upstairs; the door is locked at night, no one here to open it, so why shouldn't I lose my keys? I am wet as a dog, and a little bit hungry, just a tiny bit hungry, and a bit ridiculously tired in the knees—why shouldn't I lose the keys then? As a matter of fact, why shouldn't the whole house move out to Aker just when I came home and wanted to go in? . . . And I laughed to myself, callous from hunger and exhaustion. I heard the horses stamping in their stables, and I could see my window upstairs, but I could not open the door and I could not get in. Tired and furious, I decided therefore to return to the pier and look for my keys.

The rain had started again, and I could already feel water soaking through on my shoulders. Near the city jail I suddenly had a bright idea: I would ask the police to open the door. I went straight to a patrolman and asked him earnestly to go with me and let me in if he could.

"Yes, if I could, certainly!" But he couldn't, he didn't have any keys. The police keys were not here but in the Detective Bureau.

"What should I do then?"

"What I would do is go to a hotel and get a room."

"But I can't really go to a hotel—I haven't got an øre. I was out tonight, at a club, you understand. . . ."

We stood a little while on the steps of the jail. He thought and considered it all and looked me over. Rain poured down in the street.

"Then go to the Officer on Duty and register as homeless."

As homeless? I had never thought of that. But Christ, that was a good idea! I thanked the policeman on the spot for this excellent thought. "Could I simply go in and say that I am homeless?"

"That's all! . . ."

"Name," asked the Officer on Duty.

"Tangen—Andreas Tangen."

I don't know why I lied. Ideas were flying all about in my head, and my brain gave me more notions than I could put into use; I hit on this curious name in an instant and tossed it out without hesitation. I lied when it wasn't necessary.

"Position?"

Now he was pushing me against the wall. Hmm. I thought first of turning into a tinsmith, but didn't dare— I had given a name unusual for a tinsmith; besides, I was wearing glasses. I decided to jump in, so I took a step forward and said rapidly and solemnly: "Journalist."

The Officer on Duty gave a little start before he wrote that down, and I stood before the counter impressive as a homeless cabinet minister. He suspected nothing: the officer could understand about my hesitating a bit with my answer. What next, a journalist in the city jail, with no roof over his head!

"With which paper—Mr. Tangen?"

"With the *Morning Times*," I said. "Unfortunately, I was out tonight, a little too late, I guess. . . ."

"Well, we won't mention that!" he broke in, and went on with a smile: "When young people go out . . . we understand." He rose and bowed politely to me, saying to a policeman, "Show this gentleman up to the reserved section. Good night."

My boldness made a cold chill go over my back, and I clenched my hands as I walked, to stiffen myself a little.

"The gas light will burn for ten minutes," the policeman said from the door.

"And then it goes out?"

"Then it goes out."

I sat on my bed and listened to the key being turned. The bright cell looked friendly; I felt snug and lucky indoors and listened with pleasure to the rain outside. How could I wish for anything better than this cozy cell? My contentment grew—sitting on the bed with my head in my hands and eyes fixed on the gas lamp on the wall, I took to going over the events in my first involvement with the police. This was the first, and I had carried it off! Mr. Tangen, the journalist, I beg your pardon. . . . And then the *Morning Times!* I had really stuck him in the heart with that *Morning Times!* Well, we won't mention that, eh? Sat in evening clothes in an expensive club until 2 a.m., forgot the doorkeys and his billfold (holding several thousand) at home! Show this gentleman up to the reserved section. . . .

The gas suddenly went off, so suddenly it was strange—no dwindling, no flickering. I sat in a deep darkness. I couldn't even see my hand, or the white walls around me, nothing. There was nothing to do but to go to bed. So I undressed.

I still was not sleepy, however, and could not fall asleep. I remained a while looking into the dark—this dense substance of darkness that had no bottom, which I couldn't understand. My thoughts could not grasp such a thing. It seemed to be dark beyond all measurement, and I felt its presence weigh me down. I closed my eyes and took to singing half aloud and rocking myself back and forth on the cot to amuse myself, but it did no good. The dark had captured my brain and gave me not an instant of peace. What if I myself became dissolved into the dark, turned into it? I sat up in bed and struck out with my arms.

My nervous condition had completely taken over, and no amount of struggle against it helped. I sat there, a prey to the weirdest fantasies, gurgling to myself, humming lullabies, sweating in my effort to be calm. I stared out into the dark, and had never in all my life seen such blackness. There was no doubt that what I was faced with here was a special kind of blackness, an extreme element which no one before had ever noticed. The most ridiculous ideas occupied me, and everything frightened me. The tiny hole in the wall by my bed bothered me a great deal—a nail hole I found, a gouge in the wall. I felt of it, blew into it to try to guess its depth. It wasn't just an innocent hole, that was very clear—it was obviously a complicated and secretive hole that I had to be careful of. Dominated entirely by thoughts of this hole, driven out of my mind by curiosity and fear, I finally had to get out of bed and fumble for my knife blade so I could measure its depth and convince myself it didn't go all the way into the next cell.

I got back in bed to try to sleep, but actually I started again to fight against the darkness. The rain outdoors had stopped and I could not hear a sound. For a long time I lay listening for footsteps on the street, and listened hard until I had heard one passer-by, a policeman, to judge by the sound. All at once I snapped my fingers a couple of times and laughed. Hellfire and damnation! I suddenly imagined I had discovered a new word! I sat up in bed, and said: It is not in the language, I have discovered it—*Kuboaa*. It has letters just like a real word, by sweet Jesus, man, you have discovered a word! . . . *Kuboaa* . . . of tremendous linguistic significance.

The word stood out clearly in front of me in the dark.

I sat with wide eyes astonished at my discovery, laughing with joy. Then I fell to whispering: they could very well be spying on me, and I must act so as to keep my invention secret. I had arrived at the joyful insanity hunger was: I was empty and free of pain, and my thoughts no longer had any check. I debated everything silently with myself. My thoughts took amazing leaps as I tried to establish the meaning of my new word. It needn't mean either *God* or the *Tivoli Gardens,* and who had said it had to mean *cattle show?* I clenched my fists hard and repeated again: Who said it had to mean *cattle show?* When I thought it over, it was in fact not even necessary that it mean *padlock* or *sunrise.* In a word like that it was very easy to find meaning. I would just wait and see. In the meantime, I would sleep on it.

I lay back on the cot and chuckled, but said nothing, did not commit myself either for or against. Some time went by and I remained excited, the new word plagued me incessantly, kept on returning, finally took control of my thoughts entirely and made me sober down. I had formulated my opinion on what the word did not mean, but I had not yet come to a decision on what it *did* mean. "That is a secondary matter!" I said aloud to myself, and grabbed myself by the arm and repeated that it was a secondary matter. The word, thanks to God, has been discovered and that was the main thing. But thoughts pestered me constantly and kept me from falling asleep: nothing seemed to me good enough for this remarkable word. Finally I sat up a second time in bed, took my head between both hands, and said, "No, no, that is exactly what is impossible—letting it mean *emigration* or *tobacco factory!* If it could have meant something like that, I would have made the decision a long time ago and taken the consequences." No, the word was actually intended to mean something spiritual, a feeling, a state of mind—if I could only understand it? And I thought and thought to find something spiritual. It occurred to me that someone was talking, butting into my chat, and I answered angrily: "I beg your pardon? For an idiot, you are all alone in the field! *Yarn?* Go to hell!" Why should I be obligated to let it mean *yarn* when I had a special aversion to its meaning *yarn?* I had discovered the word myself, and I was perfectly within my rights to let it mean whatever I wanted it to, for that matter. So far as I knew, I had not yet committed myself. . . .

But my brain sank deeper and deeper in chaos. At last I leaped out of bed to find the water faucet. I wasn't thirsty, but my head was feverish and I felt an instinctive need for water. When I had drunk, I lay down again on the bed and decided that come hell or high water I would sleep. I closed my eyes and forced myself to be calm. I lay there several minutes without moving a muscle, I started to sweat and felt my blood hurtling through my veins. No, it was fantastic, wonderful that he should look in the paper cone for money! He coughed, you know, only once. Could he be still walking around down there! Sitting on my bench? . . . Bluish mother-of-pearl. . . . Ships. . . .

I opened my eyes. How could I keep them closed when I couldn't sleep! The same darkness was brooding around me, the same fathomless black eternity which my intelligence fought against and could not grasp. What could I compare it to? I made the wildest, most desperate efforts to find a word black enough to suit that darkness, a word so hideously black that it would blacken my mouth when I said it. God in heaven, how black it was! And I started again to think about the harbor, the ships, the dark monsters who lay waiting for me. They wanted to pull me to themselves and hold me fast and sail with me over land and sea, through dark kingdoms no man had ever seen. I felt myself on board ship, drawn on through waters, floating in clouds, going down, down. . . . I gave a hoarse shriek of fear, and hugged the bed; I had been on such a perilous journey, fallen down through the sky like a shot. How good and saved I felt when I grabbed the hard sides of the cot! That is what it is like to die, I said to myself, now I will die! Then I sat up in bed and asked intensely, "Who said that I will die? Haven't I found the word myself, and haven't I the right to decide what it is going to mean?" . . . I heard myself raving, could hear it while I was still talking. My madness was a delirium from faintness and exhaustion, but I still had my wits. Then a thought shot through my brain—I had become insane.

Possessed by terror, I got out of bed. I reeled over to the door and tried to open it, threw myself a couple of times against it to force it, knocked my head against the wall, moaned aloud, bit my fingers, cried and swore. . . .

It was all quiet; only my own voice came rolling back from the walls. I had fallen on the floor, not able any longer to lurch around the cell. Lying there, I saw something far up, right in front of my eyes, a grayish rectangle on the wall, a shade of white in it, a touch—it was daylight. Oh, how wonderfully I breathed then! I threw myself flat on the floor and wept with joy over this blessed gleam of light, sobbed with gratitude, kissed the window, and behaved like a madman. And at that moment I knew very well what I was doing. All my despair was suddenly gone, all depression and pain ended, and so far as my thoughts could discover, I did not have then a single frustrated desire. I sat up straight on the floor, folded my hands, and waited patiently for the break of day.

What a night this had been! That no one had heard the noise surprised me. But I was, of course, in the reserved section, high above the prisoners. A homeless cabinet minister, if I may be so bold. Going on in the highest spirits, I turned my eyes toward the window that grew lighter and lighter, I amused myself by imitating a cabinet minister—I called myself Von Tangen, and gave my speech in ministerial style. My fantasizing had not stopped, I was simply much less excited. Leaving the wallet in my residence was an oversight on my part which I sincerely regret! Might I have the honor to show his honor, the cabinet minister, to his bed? Then, in the greatest seriousness, with many ceremonial touches, I went to the cot and lay down.

By now it was light enough so I could recognize some of the outlines of the cell, and a little later I could make out the heavy handle on the door. That entertained me; the monotonous darkness, so maddeningly dense that it kept me from seeing myself, was broken. My blood became more quiet, and soon I felt my eyes close.

I was wakened by a couple of thumps on my door. I leaped to my feet and dressed hurriedly; my clothes were still wet from the night before.

"Report downstairs to the Officer of the Day," said a policeman.

Good Lord, was there still some red tape to go through! I thought, frightened.

I came down into a large room where thirty or forty men were sitting, all homeless. One by one they were called up by the clerk, and one by one given a meal ticket. The Officer of the Day said constantly to the policeman at his side, "Did he get a ticket? Don't forget to give them tickets. They look as if they could use a meal."

I stood looking at these tickets, and wanted one for myself.

"Andreas Tangen, journalist!"

I stepped forward and bowed.

"My dear man, what are *you* doing here?"

I explained the whole situation, gave the same story as the night before, lied through my teeth, lied with great frankness: was out a little too late, I'm afraid, lost my doorkeys. . . .

"I see," he said, and smiled. "So that is it! Did you sleep well?"

"Like a cabinet minister!" I answered. "Like a cabinet minister!"

"I am pleased at that!" he said, standing. "Good morning!"

I turned and left.

A ticket, ticket for me, too! I hadn't eaten for three endless days and nights. A loaf of bread! But no one offered me a ticket and I didn't dare ask for one. That would have caused suspicion instantly. They would have wanted to poke around in my private affairs and find out who I really was—then they would arrest me for giving false information. With my head high, millions in stocks and bonds, and my hands clasped beneath my coattails, I departed from the city jail.

The sun was already warm, it was ten, and the traffic on Youngstorvet Street was going full blast. Where should

80

I go now? I slapped my pocket to make sure my manuscript was there—when it was eleven I would go to see the editor. I stood awhile on the steps watching life go by on the street; meanwhile my clothes began to dry off. Hunger came back, gnawing me in the chest, sending sudden shoots and delicate pinpricks that hurt. Did I really have not one friend, not one acquaintance I could go to? I rummaged through my memory for a man worth ten øre and found none. Anyway, it was a lovely day all in all; sun and light poured down around me; the clear heavens flowed like a gentle sea over the Lier Hills off there. . . .

Without realizing it, I was on the way home.

I was truly starving, and along the street I found a sliver of wood to chew on. That helped. Strange I hadn't thought of that before!

The door was open, the boy who worked in the stable said good morning as usual.

"Fine weather!" he said.

"Yes," I answered. That was all I found to say. Could I possibly ask him to lend me a krone? He would certainly do it if he had it. Besides, I had once written a letter for him.

He stood, thinking over something he wanted to say.

"Fine weather it is. Hmmm. I have to pay the landlady today. Could you lend me five kroner, I wonder? Just for a few days? You helped me once before."

"No, Jens, I really can't. Not now. Maybe later, though, later today." And I staggered on up the stairs to my room.

There I threw myself down on the bed and laughed. What incredible luck that he asked me first! My honor was saved. Five kroner. God help us! You could just as well have asked me for five shares in the Steam Kitchen, or for an estate out in Aker.

The thought of those five kroner started me laughing louder and louder. What a solid type I was! Five kroner! Here's a real man for you! My sense of the ridiculous grew stronger, and I gave in to it: ugh— How this place smells of cooking! Ever since lunch this strong smell of hamburger steak, awful! And I pushed open the window to get this frightful smell out. Waiter, roast beef! Facing the table, this rickety table I had to support with my knees while I was writing, I bowed deeply and asked, "May I inquire if you would like a glass of wine?" "No?" "I am Tangen, the cabinet minister. Unfortunately I've been out a bit too late . . . keys. . . ."

Without any check, my thoughts again took off on their wild course. I was aware all the time that I was talking gibberish, and I didn't speak a single word without hearing and understanding it. I said to myself: Now you are talking gibberish again! And I couldn't help it. It was like being awake while you talk in your sleep. My brain was calm, without aches or any pressure, and my mood was clear and cloudless. I sailed off, and I made no move to stop myself.

Come in! Yes, just come in! You can see, entirely of ruby! Ylayali! Ylayali! The red soft sofa of silk! She is breathing so rapidly! Kiss me, my darling, again, again. Your arms are amber, your mouth is burning. . . . Waiter, I asked for roast beef. . . .

The sun shone in my window, downstairs I could hear the horses chewing their oats. I sat gumming my wood chip, gay, happy as a child. I constantly felt for my manuscript; I never thought consciously of it, but my instinct told me of it, my blood reminded me. Finally I pulled it out.

It had gotten wet, so I spread it out and left it in the sun. Then I started walking up and down my room. How depressing it all was! Small tin shavings lay scattered all over the floor, but there was no chair to sit in, not even a nail in the bare walls. Everything had been taken down to "Uncle" and used up. A few dozen sheets of paper on the table, covered with a heavy layer of dust, were my sole possessions; the old green blanket on the bed was lent to me a couple of months ago by Hans Pauli . . . Hans Pauli! I snapped my fingers. Hans Pauli Pettersen would help me! I tried to remember his address. How could I have forgotten Hans! He would certainly be furious that I hadn't come to him first thing. I grabbed my hat, gathered up my manuscript, and hurried down the stairs.

"Jens," I shouted into the stalls, "I'm positive I'll be able to do something for you this afternoon!"

I saw by the clock at the city jail that it was past eleven, so I decided to go to the newspaper immediately. Outside the editor's door I stopped to make sure my pages were in the right order; I smoothed them out carefully, stuck them back in my pocket, and knocked. I could hear my heart thumping as I walked in.

Scissors was at work as usual. I asked timidly after the editor. No answer. Scissors was sitting with a pair of long shears on the hunt for small bits of news in the country papers.

I repeated my question and stepped nearer.

"The editor is not here yet," Scissors finally said, without looking up.

"When do you expect him?"

"Couldn't say, couldn't say at all."

"How late will the office be open?"

To this I got no answer, and I had to leave. Scissors had not even glanced at me the whole time; he had heard my voice and recognized me from that. You are in so well here, I thought, that they don't even bother to answer you. Maybe the editor had told him to do that? It was true that ever since he had accepted my famous little article for ten kroner I had flooded him with work, ran to his door nearly every day with unusable pieces he had to read through and return. Maybe he wanted to put an end to it, give me hints to stay away. . . . I started off in the direction of the Homan district, where Pettersen lived.

Hans Pauli Pettersen was a farmer's son, living in the attic of a five-story house, Hans Pauli Pettersen was therefore poor. But if he had a krone, he wouldn't be stingy with it. I would get it as certainly as if I were holding it right now. So I walked along, rejoicing over this krone the whole way, convinced I would soon have it. When I arrived, the street door was locked and I had to ring.

"I would like to see Mr. Pettersen, the student," I said, and started to go in. "I know his room."

"Pettersen?" the girl repeated. "Is he the one who used to live in the attic? He has moved." She didn't know exactly where, but he had asked them to send his letters on to Hermansen on Toldbod Street, and she gave the number.

I walked all the way down to Toldbod Street full of hope and faith to ask for Hans Pauli's address. It was my last chance, I had to reach for it. On the way I passed a new house in front of which a couple of carpenters were planing. From the pile I took a couple of shiny shavings, put one in my mouth, and saved the other in my pocket for later. I walked on. I moaned from hunger. In a baker's window I had seen an incredible immense loaf for ten øre, the largest loaf one could buy for that price. . . .

"I've come to find out where Mr. Pettersen, the student, lives."

"Bernt Ankers Street, number 10, attic." Was I possibly going there? If so, would I be so good as to take along a couple of letters that were here?

I walked up to the main part of the city again, the same road I had taken down, passing the carpenters who were sitting now with their lunch pails between their knees eating good warm food from the Steam Kitchen, passing the bakery window where the loaf was still lying, and finally reached Bernt Ankers Street half dead with exhaustion. The door was open, and I trudged up the heavy stairs to the attic. I took the letters from my pocket so that I could give them to Hans Pauli as soon as I went in, and put him in a good mood with one crack. He would never never refuse his help when I told him my situation, not Hans, never, he had such a big heart, I had always said that about him. . . . On the door I found his card: "H. P. Pettersen. Student of Theology. —Gone home for vacation."

I sat down on the spot, sat on the bare floor, tired beyond belief, exhausted and defeated. I repeated mechanically two or three times: "Gone home!" "Gone home!" Then I lapsed into utter silence. There wasn't a tear in my eyes, I didn't have a thought or a feeling. With eyes wide open I sat staring at the letters without doing a thing. Ten minutes went by, perhaps twenty or more. I sat there in the same place, not moving a finger. This dull stupor was almost like a nap. At last I heard someone coming up the stairs; I stood up and said, "I'm looking for Mr. Pettersen, the student—I have two letters here for him."

"He has gone home," the woman replied. "But he will be back after the holidays. I can take the letters, if you want me to."

"Oh, thank you, that would be a great help," I said. "He will get them then when he comes. They could be important. Good morning."

When I was outside, I stopped and said aloud in the middle of the street with clenched fists: "I will tell you one thing, my dear Lord and God: you are a you-know-what!" Then I nodded furiously and repeated through clenched teeth up toward the clouds: "I swear to God you are a you-know-what!"

I walked several steps and then stopped again. Suddenly changing my whole posture, I folded my hands, twisted my head over to the side a little, and asked in a soft sanctimonious voice: "Have you taken your troubles to him, my child?"

That didn't sound right.

"Capital H," I said. "H as big as a cathedral!" Once more. "Have you called upon Him, my child?" Then I lowered my head and made my voice sorrowful and answered, "No."

That didn't sound right either.

You can't lie, you moron! Yes, you should have said, yes, I have called out to my God and my Father! And then you have to get the right tone in your words, the most soupy, mournful tune you have ever heard. O.K., once more! Ah, that was better. But you have to sigh, sigh, like a horse with colic. That's the idea!

So I walked along giving myself advice, and stamping impatiently when I didn't take it, and scolding myself as a blockhead while astonished passers-by turned around to watch me.

I sucked on my wood shaving without stopping, and

staggered on up the street as rapidly as I could. Before I knew it, I was all the way down to the market square by the railway station.

The clock on the Church of Our Saviour showed one-thirty. I stood awhile, thinking. I felt a faint sweat on my face which trickled into my eyes. Would you be interested in a walk down to the pier? I said to myself. I mean, only, of course, if you can spare the time? I bowed to myself, and walked down to the railway station pier.

The ships lay off the piers, the sea was rocking in the sunshine. Everywhere there was busyness, steam whistles shrieking, longshoremen with boxes on their shoulders, cheerful loading songs from the barges. A cake seller was sitting near me, with her brown nose leaning over her merchandise: the tiny board in front of her was wickedly full of cakes, and I turned away with effort. The odor from her merchandise was filling the entire wharf—ugh! open the windows! I turned to the man sitting next to me, and put the case to him forcibly about the disproportionate number of cake sellers around, cake sellers here, there, everywhere—no? Well, surely he had to admit . . . But the dear man smelled trouble and didn't let me finish before he stood up and left. I stood up too, and followed him, determined to point out to him his error.

"Thinking of sanitary considerations alone," I said, and put my hand on his shoulder. . . .

"Pardon me, I am a stranger and I don't know anything about sanitary considerations," he said, and looked at me in fright.

"Well, if you are a stranger, that changes everything. . . . Could I be of any help to you? Show you around? No, sure? That would be a pleasure for me, and it wouldn't cost you a thing. . . ."

He wanted badly to get rid of me, however, and walked hurriedly across the street to the other sidewalk.

I went back to my bench and sat down. I was very nervous and the large street organ that had started playing down the street made it worse. A rapid mechanical music, some fragment of Weber, to which a small girl was singing a mournful song. The sorrowful, flutelike sound of the organ shivered in me, my nerves began to vibrate like a sounding board, and an instant later I slumped backward on the bench, whining and humming with the music. What odd things the feelings stuck to when one was hungry! I felt drawn up by the notes, dissolved in them, I began to flow out into the air, and could see very clearly what I was flowing over, high over mountains, dancing on in waves over brilliant areas. . . .

"One øre!" the little organ grinder's daughter said, and stretched out her tin plate, "only one øre!"

"Yes!" I answered mechanically, and leaped up, rummaging in my pocket. The child, however, thought I was only mocking her, and backed off without saying a word. This speechless humility was too much for me; if she had scolded at me, I would have liked it better. Pain shot through me and I called her to come back. "I don't have a single øre," I said. "But I'll give you something later, in the morning perhaps. What is your name? That is a very nice name, I won't forget that. Till tomorrow then. . . ."

I knew that she hadn't believed me, even though she had not said a word, and I cried out with despair because this tiny waif had refused to believe me. At the end I called her back once more, ripped off my suitcoat, and was about to give her my waistcoat. "I'll make it all good," I said. "Wait just a minute. . . ."

I had no waistcoat!

How could I be looking for it then! It had been weeks since I owned it! What was the matter with me? The astonished girl waited no longer, she carefully drew back and left. And I had to let her go. People gathered around me, laughing aloud, a policeman forced his way in to me and wanted to know what was going on.

"Nothing," I answered, "nothing at all! I was only trying to give that girl over there my waistcoat . . . for her father. . . . You don't have to stand around laughing about that. All I have to do is go home and put on another."

"No disturbing of the peace!" said the policeman. "So,

move along now!" And he pushed me away. "Is this your stuff?" he shouted after me.

"Yes, my God, my newspaper article, papers, important ones! How could I have been so careless?"

I grabbed my manuscript, checked to see that it was in the right order, and walked without pausing or even looking around me to the newspaper office. The clock on Our Saviour's said four.

The office was closed. I slipped silently down the stairs, frightened as a thief, and stood at loose ends outside on the street. What should I do now? I leaned against the building, stared down at the sidewalk, and thought. A safety pin lay glittering by my feet; I bent down and picked it up. What if I took off my coat buttons, how much would I get for them? Maybe there was no sense to it. Buttons were buttons, though on examining them from all sides I saw they were as good as new. In any case, it was well worth trying, I could take my knife blade, slit them off, and cart them away to the pawnbroker. The hope of selling these five buttons cheered me up instantly, and I said: "See, it's all going to come out all right!" My joy overpowered me, and I immediately started cutting the buttons off, one after the other. All that time, I kept up a silent chatter with myself:

"Well, you see, a man becomes a bit pressed for money, just temporary of course. . . . Worn out, you say? You mustn't make reckless statements. Just show me someone who wears out fewer buttons than I do. I wear my coat open all the time, that's the truth; it's become a quirk of mine, a habit. . . . No no, if you don't *want* to. But I must have ten øre for them at the very least. . . . God in heaven, who said you *had* to do it? You can just shut up and leave me alone. . . . All right, all right, go and *get* the police then. I'll wait here while you're looking for a policeman. And I won't steal a thing from you. . . . Yes, good day! Good day! My name actually is Tangen, I've been out a little too late. . . ."

Someone was coming down the stairs. I returned in a second to reality, recognized Scissors, and put the buttons carefully in my pocket. He tried to go by, didn't answer my greeting, suddenly became very occupied in looking at his fingernails. I stopped him and inquired after the editor.

"He is out."

"You are lying!" I said. Then, with an audacity that surprised even myself, I continued: "I have to talk with him; it is urgent. I have some information from the Governor's Mansion."

"Can't you just tell it to me?"

"To you?" I said, and passed a withering eye over him. It helped. He walked straight back up the stairs and unlocked the door. My heart was in my mouth. I clenched my teeth hard to give me courage, knocked, and walked into the editor's private office.

"It's you! Good day!" he said cheerfully. "Sit down."

If he had ordered me out right away, it would have been easier; I felt near crying, and said, "Forgive me for . . ."

"Sit yourself down," he repeated.

So I sat down and explained that I had a piece I felt strongly about seeing in his paper. I had worked on it with tremendous diligence, it had cost me considerable labor.

"I will read it," he said, taking it. "Of course everything you write will cost you labor; the only trouble with your work perhaps is excitability. If you could only be a little more composed! There is too much fever all the time. Anyway, I'll read it." Then he turned again to his desk work.

There I sat. Did I dare ask him for a krone? Explain to him why there was fever all the time? He would be certain to help me; he had done it before.

I stood up. Hmm! The last time I was here he had grumbled about the lack of cash and had finally sent a messenger out to scrape up some for me. Maybe it would be the same thing now. That would be bad. Couldn't I see in the first place that he was working?

"Was there anything else?" he asked.

"No!" I said, and made my voice strong. "When should I stop in again?"

"Oh, whenever it's convenient," he answered. "A couple of days or so."

I couldn't get my application past my lips. The friendliness of this man seemed to me beyond description, and I ought to know how to appreciate it. Better to starve to death. So I left.

Not once, not even when I was outside again and felt the hunger return, did I repent having left the office without asking for that krone. I took the second wood shaving out of my pocket and put it in my mouth. It helped once more. Why hadn't I done that before? Shame on you! I said aloud. Could you actually have thought of asking this man for a krone and embarrassing him a second time? And I grew downright angry with myself for the shamelessness I was almost guilty of. "By God, that was the shabbiest thing I ever heard of!" I said. "Rushing at a man and nearly clawing his eyes out just because you want a krone, you worthless dog! Go on, then, march! Faster! Faster, you clod! I'll teach you!"

I began running so as to punish myself, left street after street behind me, pushed myself on with inward jeers, and screeched silently and furiously at myself whenever I felt like stopping. With the help of these exertions I ended up far along Pile Street. When I finally did stop, almost weeping with anger that I couldn't run any farther, my whole body trembled, and I threw myself down on a house stoop. "Not so fast!" I said. And to torture myself right, I stood up again and forced myself to stand there, laughing at myself, and gloating over my own fatigue. Finally, after a few minutes, I nodded and so gave myself permission to sit down; however, I chose the most uncomfortable spot on the stoop.

Lord, Lord, how wonderful it was to rest! I dried the sweat from my face, and drew in huge clean breaths of air. How I had run! But I didn't regret it, I deserved it. Why had I ever wanted to ask for that krone? There you see the results! So I started talking gently to myself, delivering advice as a mother might do. I became moved, more and more; tired and weak, I started crying—a silent, inner crying, an interior sobbing without a tear.

For a quarter of an hour or more I sat there. People came and went, and no one bothered me. Small children played around me, a tiny bird sang in a tree on the other side of the street.

A policeman came over to me and said, "Why are you sitting here?"

"Why am I sitting here?" I asked. "For fun."

"I've been watching you the last half hour," he said. "You've been sitting here nearly a half hour?"

"About that," I answered. "So what?" I stood up angry and left.

Back at the market, I stopped and looked down at the street. For fun! What sort of an answer was that? From exhaustion, you should have said, and then you should have made your voice all tearful—you are a lunkhead, you will never learn to be a real hypocrite! From exhaustion and fatigue! And you should have sighed like a horse.

When I passed the firehouse I stopped again, possessed by a new whim. I snapped my fingers, gave out a loud laugh that astounded the passers-by, and said, "What you should do is to go out to Pastor Levison's! By God and hell, that is what you shall do. Well, it won't hurt to try. What have you got to lose? Besides, it's such marvelous weather."

I went into Pascha's Bookstore, found his address in a directory, and started out there. "Now this is serious!" I said. "No idiotic tricks! Conscience, you say? No rubbish —you are too poor to have a conscience! You are hungry, hungry, this is a grave matter now, this is urgent! But you have to twist your head to the side and get some music in your voice. You don't want to? All right, then, I won't go a step farther with you, and you can get that straight. Now: you are sorely troubled, you have been battling with the Powers of Darkness, with silent monsters in the darkness, a darkness so immense that one gets the horrors just thinking of it, you hunger and thirst after wine and milk, and receive them not. That is the state that you are in. Now you stand here, not worth a tinker's dam. However, you do believe in grace, thank the Lord for that, you still have not lost your faith! The next thing is to fold your hands together and show you are a real crackerjack at believing in grace! With respect to Mammon, you hate Mammon in all his works and all his ways; with a psalmbook, it is another matter entirely—a couple of kroner, as a token, to remember this." . . . I stopped short and read on the minister's door: "Office Hours: 12–4."

"No nonsense now!" I said. "This has to be serious! O.K., down with the head, a little more. . . ." I rang at his house door.

"I am looking for the pastor," I said to the girl who answered, though I couldn't make myself put in the name of God, too.

"He is not here," she answered.

Not here! Not here! That demolished my plan, completely destroyed everything I had intended to say. What good had I gotten from this long walk? I stood there.

"Was it something special?" asked the girl.

"No, no!" I answered. "Certainly not! It was just that God has sent us such marvelous weather, and I wanted to walk out and say hello."

I stood there and she stood there. I carefully pushed my chest out so that she would notice the safety pins holding my suitcoat together; I begged her with my eyes to see what I had come for; but she, poor thing, understood nothing at all.

"Yes, wonderful weather. Is the pastor's wife at home, I wonder?"

"She is, but she has arthritis and has to lie on the sofa and can't move around. . . ." Would I perhaps like to leave a message or something?

"No, thank you. I take walks like this now and then, get a little exercise. After lunch the air was so clear."

I started back. What was the sense of chattering any more? Besides, I was beginning to feel a dizziness: no question of it, I was heading for a collapse, a real one. Office Hours: 12–4. I had knocked an hour too late: grace hour is over!

At the main market I sat down on one of the benches

near the church. God in heaven, how black it was starting to look around me! I was too tired to cry, my last bit of energy was gone, I just sat there without ideas or plans, sat motionless and starved. My chest burned the most, an evil sort of smarting went on in there all the time. Chewing the shaving no longer did any good either; my teeth were tired of their fruitless labor, and I let them rest. I gave up. On top of it all, a piece of brownish orange peel I had found on the street and immediately started gnawing on made me nauseated. I was sick; my pulse swelled up bluish on my wrists.

What actually was I waiting for? I had run around the whole day after one krone in order to stay alive a few more hours. What was the difference, really, if what was inevitable happened one day earlier or one day later? If I had been behaving like a reasonable man, I would have gone home and lain down quietly a long time ago, just given up. For an instant my brain was utterly clear. I was going to die; fall had come and everything was ready to hibernate. I had tried every way out, used every possible means I knew of. I hugged that idea with sentimentality and every time I thought hopefully of a possible way out, I whispered, nay-saying: "You fool, you, your whole body has started to die!" What I should do is to write a few letters, get everything ready, and have myself prepared. I would get myself clean, and make my bed; I would lay my head on my pile of writing paper, the purest thing I had left, and I could put the green blanket. . . .

The green blanket! At one stroke I was wide awake, my blood rose to my brain, and my heart gave a leap. I stood up and started walking, I felt full of life again, and I repeated over and over the disjointed words: The green blanket! The green blanket! I walked faster and faster as if it were a question of going back for something, and in a few minutes I was home again in my tinsmith's shop.

Without pausing a moment or weakening in my decision, I walked over to the bed and rolled up Hans Pauli's blanket. If this bright idea doesn't save me, it will be strange! The stupid misgivings that appeared in me I rose infinitely above; I said goodbye to the whole bunch. I was no hero, I was not virtue's fool, I had all my wits. . . .

Then I put the blanket under my arm and went to 5 Steners Street.

I knocked and walked into the large, unfamiliar room for the first time; the bells over the door made a whole flock of desperate clangs above me. A man entered from a side room chewing, his mouth full of food, and took his place behind the counter.

"Could you lend me a half krone on my glasses?" I said. "I'll redeem them in a couple of days, for sure."

"What? But aren't they steel-rimmed?"

"Yes."

"No, I can't do it."

"Well, no, you're probably right. It was really just a joke. But here I've got a blanket which I really haven't any use for any more, and I thought you might be able to take it off my hands."

"Unfortunately I have an entire storeroom full of bed-clothes," he answered. When I got it unrolled, he glanced at it and said loudly, "You have to excuse me, I can't possibly use that either!"

"I wanted to show you the worst side first," I said. "It is much better on the other side."

"No, no, that won't make any difference, I don't want it, and you will never get ten øre for it anywhere!"

"I know it isn't worth anything," I said, "but I thought it might go if it were sold with another old blanket at an auction."

"No, no, it won't do."

"Twenty-five øre?" I said.

"Listen, I won't have it, I don't want it on my premises!" So I put the blanket under my arm again and went home. I acted as though nothing had happened, spread the blanket out again on the bed, smoothed out the wrinkles as I always did, and tried to erase every trace of my last action. I couldn't possibly have been in my right mind when I decided to try this filthy trick. The more I thought of it, the more irrational it seemed. It must have been a sudden attack of weakness, some failure of energy far inside that had caught me off guard. I hadn't just fallen in the snare with closed eyes either, I had sensed that something was going wrong on the spot, and I had explicitly attempted first with the glasses, and I was so glad that I hadn't been able to commit this sin which would have stained the last hours of my life.

I wandered out again on the street.

I sat down once more on a bench near the Church of Our Saviour, dozed with my head on my chest, limp again after the recent excitement, sick and fatigued from hunger. Time went by.

I managed to sit the hour out; it was a bit lighter outside than inside the house; it struck me also that the pain in my chest was not so wild out of doors. I would get back to my room soon enough anyway.

So I dozed and thought and felt sharp pains. I had found a tiny stone, which I polished and stuck in my mouth to have something to chew on; otherwise I didn't move a muscle, not even my eyes. People came and went. Wagon noise, noise of horses, and chatter filled the air.

Of course I could try the buttons? It wouldn't do any good, naturally, and besides I was really sick. But when I thought of it, wouldn't I actually go almost past "Uncle" —my private "Uncle"—on the way home?

Finally I stood up and slowly walked and staggered along the street. I began to feel a burning above my eyebrows, it was fever coming, and I hurried on as fast as I could. I passed the bakery where the loaf of bread was on display. Now, I said with elaborate decisiveness, we are not stopping here! But suppose I just went in and asked for a piece of bread? That was only an idea, a passing thought. Ugh! I whispered, shaking my head. I walked on looking at myself ironically. I knew very well that it was no use to expect anything free from that shop.

On Repslager Street, two lovers were standing in a doorway whispering; farther down, a girl stuck her head out of the window. I was walking so slowly and thoughtfully that I appeared to have a lot of different things on my mind—so the girl came out of the house.

"How're you doing today, honey? Oh, my God, are you sick? What's wrong with your face?" She hurried back into the house.

I stopped. What *was* wrong with my face? Had I actually started dying? I felt my cheeks: Thin, naturally I was thin: my cheeks were as concave as two bowls—God in heaven! I pushed on.

But then I stopped once more. I must be unbelievably thin. My eyes would soon be all the way through my head. I wonder how I actually look? What in the hell is going on that a man has to turn himself into a living freak out of sheer hunger? I felt rage one more time, its final flaring up, a muscular spasm. "What's wrong with your face, eh?" Here I was walking around with a better head than anyone else in the country, and a pair of fists that could, so help me God, grind a longshoreman into small bits, into powder, and I was becoming a freak from hunger in the middle of the city of Christiania! Was there any sense or reason in that? I had slept in the harness and worked day and night like a minister's mare; I had read till my eyes fell out of their sockets, and starved my hairs out of my head—and in hell's name, what for? Even whores on the street fled so as not to have to look at me. But now that was going to stop—do you hear me—*stop*, and hell take the whole thing! . . . With steadily increasing rage, I ground my teeth in despair, and with sobs and oaths I went on and roared wildly, paying no attention to the people going by. I started once more to punish my flesh, ran my forehead deliberately against lampposts, drove my fingernails deep into the backs of my hands, bit my tongue madly every time it failed to pronounce clearly and then laughed wildly whenever I caused a fairly good pain.

Yes, but what shall I do? I finally said to myself. Then I stamped on the sidewalk several times, repeating, What shall I do?

A man walking past me said with a smile: "You could go and ask them to lock you up."

I looked after him. It was a well-known lady-killer whom everyone called "The Duke." Not even he understood my condition, a man I knew, whose hand I had shaken. I stopped still. Locked up? Well, I was mad, that was true. I felt insanity in my blood, I felt it rushing through my brain. So that is where I will end? Yes, yes! I started my slow, mournful walk again. That was where my ship would tie up!

Suddenly I stopped short again. But not locked up! I said, not that! And I got almost hoarse with fear. I begged on my own behalf, beseeched the air and the sky not to be locked up. Then I would go to the city jail again, be imprisoned in a dark cell where there wasn't even a glimmer of light. Not that! There were other ways out that I hadn't tried yet. And I would try them; I would be more diligent, spend much more time on it, and go doggedly around from house to house. There was the music seller Cisler, for example. I had not tried him. There was surely some way. . . . I walked on, talking this way until I got myself crying once more from emotion. Only not to be locked up!

Cisler? Was that perhaps a sign to me from higher powers? His name had occurred to me, suddenly, for no reason at all, and he actually lived some distance away: I would look him up anyway, walk slowly and rest once in a while. I knew the store, I had been there often, and bought a little music there in the old days. Should I ask him for a half krone? That might embarrass him, better to ask for a whole krone.

I entered the shop and inquired for the manager; they showed me into his office. There he sat, handsome, dressed in the latest style, looking through some papers.

I stammered, excuse me, and stated my errand. Forced by need to turn to him. . . . Wouldn't be very long before I could pay him back. . . . As soon as I was paid for my article in the paper. . . . If he would do me such a great favor. . . .

Even while I was talking, he turned back to his desk and went on with his work. When I was through, he looked up at me sideways, shook his elegant head, and said, No! No sort of explanation. Not a word.

My knees shook violently and I leaned against the little polished rail. I had to try once more. Why should his particular name have occurred to me when I was standing down there in Vaterland Street? I felt some twinges of pain in my left side, and I started to sweat. Hmm. "I am really very weak," I said. "Unfortunately a little ill; but certainly it would be no more than two or three days before I could pay it back. Would it be too much to ask . . .?"

"My dear fellow, why are you coming to me?" he said. "To me you are a complete blank, come in off the street. Go to the paper, where they know you."

"But only for tonight!" I said. "The office is closed now and I am extremely hungry already." He shook his head insistently and kept on shaking it even after I had taken hold of the doorknob.

"Goodbye!" I said.

That was no sign from higher powers, I thought, and smiled bitterly; I could give signs from that altitude myself if I had to. I toiled on, one block after the other, now and then resting a minute on a stoop. Just as long as I wasn't locked up! Fright of the cell accompanied me all the time and gave me no peace: every time I saw a policeman ahead, I staggered into a side street to avoid meeting him. Now we will count one hundred steps, I said, and then try our luck again! One of these times it will work.

It was a small yarn shop, a place I had never been in. A man stood behind the counter alone; farther back there was an office with a porcelain name plate on the door, and a long series of full shelves and tables. I waited until the last customer, a young woman with dimples, had left. How happy she looked! I did not try to impress this girl with the safety pins in my coat, but turned away.

"Can I help you?" asked the clerk.

"Is the manager here?" I said.

"He is on a trip in the mountains," he answered. "Was it something special?"

"It's about a few øre for food," I said, trying to smile. "I am hungry and I haven't a single øre."

"Then you are as rich as I am," he said, and began arranging packages of yarn.

"Oh, don't say no—not now!" I said, suddenly cold over my whole body. "Really, I am nearly dead from hunger, it is many days since I've eaten anything at all."

Without a word, or a trace of humor in his actions, he began one by one turning his pockets inside out. Would I take his word for it then?

"Only five øre," I said. "I'll give you ten back for it in a couple of days."

"My dear fellow, what do you want me to do, steal from the till?" he asked in an impatient voice.

"Yes!" I said. "Yes, take five øre from the till!"

"I won't be the one who does that," he said decisively, and then added, "And while we're at it, let me tell you that I think we've had enough of this."

I slumped out, sick with hunger and hot with shame. It is time all this came to an end! This thing was really going on too long. I had held myself straight for so many years, kept upright in such hard times, and now all of a sudden I had sunk to the coarsest sort of begging. This one day had brutalized my mind entirely, shamelessness had spattered me. I had even had the gall to become pathetic and stand weeping in front of the most insignificant shopkeepers. And what good had it done? Wasn't I still without even a piece of bread to stick in my mouth? I had succeeded in making me disgusting to myself. Yes, yes, this thing had to come to an end now! But they were locking the door at home already, and I had to hurry if I didn't want to spend the night in the city jail again. . . .

That deadline gave me strength—sleeping in jail I did not want to do. With my body bent over, hands pressed against my ribs on the left to dull the pain a bit, I flailed on ahead, keeping my eyes fastened to the sidewalk to avoid greetings from any possible acquaintances, and got to the firehouse. Thank God. Our Saviour's clock showed only seven o'clock, I had three hours yet before the door closed. How frightened I had been.

Anyway, not a thing had been left untried, I had done everything I could. Imagine that I hadn't had luck even once the whole day! If I told that to someone, no one would believe it; if I wrote it, everyone would swear it was invented. Not in a single place! Well, well, there was nothing to do then—most of all, don't go and be weepy again. How revolting that was! I can assure you it lowers you considerably in my estimation! If hope was gone, it was gone. I wonder if I couldn't steal a handful of oats from the stable? A flicker of light, an idea—I knew that the stable was locked.

I took it easy and crept at a slow snail's pace. I felt thirsty, luckily for the first time all day. I walked on, looking for a place to get a drink. I was a long way from the market square, and I didn't want to ask at a private house; I could wait of course until I got home—that would take fifteen minutes. Of course it wasn't at all certain I could keep down a mouthful of water either; my stomach was sensitive to everything now—I even felt nauseated from the spit I swallowed as I walked.

The buttons! I hadn't tried with the buttons yet? I stopped stock still, and started smiling. Maybe there was a solution! I was not completely finished! No question, I would get ten øre for them, tomorrow I would lay hands on ten more some place or other, and Thursday I would be paid for my newspaper article! I would see, it would be all right! Imagine forgetting the buttons! I pulled them out of my pocket and looked at them while I walked; my eyes grew dark with joy, I didn't see much of the street I was walking on.

How well I knew that large basement shop, my refuge in the dark evenings, my vampire friend! One by one, all my possessions had vanished down there, the little things I had brought from home, my last book. On the auction days I enjoyed going there to watch, and I rejoiced every time my books seemed to have found a good home. Magelsen, the actor, had my watch, and I was almost proud of that; a diary in which I had written my first little poetic ventures had been bought by an acquaintance, and my overcoat had found shelter in the closet of a photographer's studio. So I had nothing to complain about there.

I held my buttons ready in my hand, and walked in. "Uncle" was sitting at his desk, writing.

"I'm in no hurry," I said, afraid of disturbing him and putting him in a bad mood. My voice sounded so curiously hollow that I hardly recognized it myself, and my heart thumped like a hammer.

He came toward me smiling as he always did, put both his hands palm down on the counter, and looked me straight in the eye without saying anything.

"Well, I have something here, and I wanted to ask you if you had any use for—something that was really in the way at home, you understand, no room for them, some buttons."

"What was that, what was that about buttons?" And he bent his head down nearly to my hand.

Could he give me a few øre for them? . . . As much as he thought right. . . . He was the best judge of that. . . .

"For the buttons?" And "Uncle" stared at me, amazed. "For *these* buttons?"

"Just enough for a cigar or whatever you think right. I was just going by anyway and thought I'd stop in."

The old pawnbroker laughed and went back to his desk without saying a word. I stood there. I hadn't actually hoped for much, and yet I had thought it was possible I would get something. The laugh was a death sentence. I suppose the glasses wouldn't do much good either.

"Naturally I will put my glasses in with them," I said. "That goes without saying." I took them off. "Just ten øre, or if you prefer, five øre?"

"You know very well that I can't lend you anything on your glasses," "Uncle" said. "I've told you that before."

"But I need a stamp," I said dully. "I can't even mail the letter I need to send. A ten- or a five-øre stamp, whatever you think yourself."

"God bless you, be on your way now!" he answered, and shooed me out with his hands.

"All right, that's the way it will have to be!" I said to

myself. I put the glasses back on mechanically, picked up the buttons, and left. I said good night and latched the door after me as I always did. You can see, there is nothing more to be done! When I was back up on the sidewalk, I stopped and looked at the buttons once more. "That he wouldn't even take them!" I said. "They are almost new—I don't understand it at all!"

While I was making these observations to myself, a man brushed past me and started down. In passing, he had given me a little shove, we both said excuse me, and I turned around and looked after him.

"Say, is it you?" he said from down on the steps. He came back up and I recognized him. "God help us, you look terrible!" he said. "What were you doing down there?"

"Oh—had some business. You're going down there, I see."

"Yes. What did you bring to him?"

My knees shook, I leaned against the wall for support, and reached out my hand with the buttons, open.

"Holy Christ!" he shouted. "What are you doing? This is going too far."

"Goodbye!" I said, and started to go. I felt a sobbing inside me.

"No, wait a minute!" he said.

What should I wait for? He was on his way to "Uncle" himself, bringing his engagement ring, perhaps, been starving for several days, avoiding his landlady.

"Well, all right," I answered. "If you won't be too . . ."

"Of course not," he said, taking hold of my arm. "But the truth is, I don't trust you, you are an absolute idiot. You had better come right down here with me."

I knew what he had in mind, and suddenly I felt again a little ache of honor, and I answered: "Can't do it! I have to be in Bernt Ankers Street at eight-thirty, and . . ."

"Eight-thirty, that's fine! Now, it is only eight. Look at this watch, it's right here in my hand—that is what I'm going to take down. So, get in there, you starving old devil! I'll get at least five kroner for you."

And he pushed me in.

PART THREE

A week went by in joy and gladness.

I was over the worst this time again, I had food every day, my spirits rose, and I pushed one iron after the other into the fire. I had three or four essays in the works, which plundered my poor brain of every spark, every idea that occurred to it; my writing seemed to me better than it had ever been. The last article, in which I had put so much stock, for which I had so much hope, had already been returned by the editor. I tore it up immediately, angry and insulted, without even reading it over. I intended, in the future, to try another newspaper also, so as to have several outlets.

In the last resort, if everything failed, I always had the ships to turn to. *The Nun* was lying off the pier ready to sail, and I could probably sign on to go to Archangel or wherever the ship was going at the moment. So there was no lack of possibilities on many sides.

The last crisis had been hard on me: I was beginning to lose a lot of hair, headaches were also a great bother, particularly during the mornings, and my general nervousness stayed on. During the day I sat writing with my hands wrapped in rags simply because they were so sensitive that my own breath on them was painful. When Jens Olai slammed the stable doors downstairs hard, or when a dog came into the yard at the back and started to bark, the sound went right through the marrow of my bones like needles, and I felt the pain everywhere. I was in poor shape.

Day after day I toiled on my articles, taking off barely time enough to gobble down my food before I set to writing again. During those days, both the bed and my little rickety table were swimming in notes and scribbled-over manuscripts that I took turns working on, adding new ideas that occurred to me in the course of the day, crossing out material or freshening up the dead passages with a lively word here or there, and pushing on from sentence to sentence with great labor. Finally one afternoon one of my essays was finished; I put it gaily in my pocket and started off to see my editor, whom I called "the Chief." It was about time I made a move to get more money, I had not many øre left.

The Chief asked me to wait a bit, to sit down, he would be with me in a minute. . . . He went on writing.

I looked around me in the tiny office: busts, lithographs, clippings, and an enormous wastebasket that looked as if it could swallow a man, bones and all. I felt sad, looking at this monstrous maw, this dragon—mouth always open, ready to receive more rejected articles, newly crushed hopes.

"What's today's date?" the Chief suddenly asked from his desk.

"The twenty-eighth," I answered, glad to be of service to him.

"The twenty-eighth." He wrote on. Finally he found envelopes for a couple of letters, tossed some papers in the wastebasket, and looked at me. When he saw that I was still standing by the door, he made a half-serious, half-joking gesture with his hands, pointing at a chair.

I turned partly away so that he wouldn't see, as I unbuttoned my coat, that my waistcoat was missing, and I took my manuscript from my pocket.

"It is just a small sketch of Correggio," I said, "and I'm afraid it's written in the wrong style. . . ."

He took the sheets from my hand and started leafing through them. He turned to face me.

So this is how he looked, close-up, the man whose name I had heard since I was a child and whose paper had had a tremendous influence on me all my life. His hair was curly, and his fine brown eyes a trifle restless; one of his quirks was brushing his nose with his thumb every once in a while. A country preacher could not have looked more full of milk and honey than this formidable writer, whose words had always left long bloody marks wherever they fell. A strange feeling of fear and awe toward this man came over me, I felt tears coming to my eyes, and I involuntarily moved a step closer in order to tell him how much he meant to me for everything he had taught me, and to ask him not to be too hard on me—I was only a poor devil with enough troubles already.

He looked up, putting my manuscript pages slowly together again, and sat there thinking. To help him get rid of me more easily, I reached my hand out and said, "Oh, well, it's probably not usable." I smiled then, to give the impression that it wasn't very serious to me.

"Everything we use has to be popularly written. You know the kind of public we have. But I wonder if you couldn't take this and make it a little more elementary? Or else write about something that people feel more at home with?"

His consideration astounded me. I realized that my article was rejected, and yet I could not have had a more beautiful rejection. So as not to bother him any longer, I said, "Yes, I'm sure I can do that."

I walked to the door. Hmm. He had to forgive me for having wasted his time with this. . . . I bowed and reached for the knob.

"If you need it," he said, "I'd be glad to give you a small advance. You can always work it off."

Since he had just seen that my writing was unsuitable, his offer seemed slightly humiliating and I answered, "No, thanks, I'm all right for a while. But thank you very much. Goodbye!"

"Goodbye!" the Chief answered, and turned back instantly to his work.

He had treated me in any case with a courtesy I didn't deserve, and I was grateful for that: I must learn how to appreciate it. I determined not to come back until I could bring him a piece I was really satisfied with, which would take the Chief by surprise and get him to turn over ten kroner to me without thinking of it. So I walked home and set to work again.

On each of the following evenings, after the street lamps had been lit, usually about eight o'clock, a curious thing would take place.

As I left the building, after the day's labor and troubles, for a little walk in the streets, a woman dressed in black would be standing by a lamppost just outside the door; she would turn to look at me and follow me with her eyes as I walked past. I noticed that she always had the same dress on, and the same heavy veil that hid her face and fell over her breast, and that she carried a small umbrella with an ivory ring in the handle.

It was the third evening now that I had seen her, always in the same spot; as soon as I had passed, she would turn and slowly walk up the street, away from me.

My excitable brain shot out antennae, and I immediately felt sure that her visit had something to do with me. I was about to address her several times, ask her if she was looking for someone, if she needed any help, if I could walk her home, badly dressed as I was, give her some protection in these dark streets; but I had a vague fear of it all costing me something, a glass of wine, a carriage ride, and I was broke; my empty pockets had a depressing effect on me, and I didn't even have the courage to look inquiringly at her as I passed. Hunger was beginning to take hold in me again, I hadn't had any food since last night—of course, that wasn't very long, but I was beginning to weaken noticeably. I simply couldn't starve any more the way I used to. A single day without food now could make me feel dazed, and I made incessant retching efforts as soon as I drank any water. At night I got into bed fully dressed, just as I was during the day, and froze anyway, shivering with cold, and even stiffened while I slept. The old blanket could not keep out the drafts, and I woke every morning with my nose stopped up by the icy air coming in from outdoors.

I wandered around in the streets, trying to figure out how to keep going until I finished my next essay. If I only had a candle, I could try pushing on right through the night. It would only take a couple of hours once I warmed up to it—tomorrow morning I could go see the Chief again.

I walked straight into the Oplandske Café, looking for my young banker friend to scrounge ten øre for a candle. They let me go from room to room without bothering me; I walked past a dozen tables at which chattering customers sat eating and drinking, got to the back of the restaurant, even into the Red Room, without finding my man. Disappointed and irritated, I went back out on the street and drifted off in the direction of the castle.

Wasn't this great, what the hell was going on, why was there never any end to my troubles! Taking long strides, my coat collar turned brutally up to my chin, my fists clenched in my pants pockets, I walked along, cursing my unlucky stars. Not a really carefree hour for seven, eight months, not even sufficient food for a week before poverty brought me to my knees again. And into the bargain I had to go and be honorable right in the middle of my misery—what a laugh, honorable all the way through! God help us all, what a fool I had been. I started recounting to myself how I had once gone around with a bad conscience from taking Hans Pauli's blanket to the pawnshop. I laughed mockingly at my tender scrupulousness, spit contemptuously in the street, and couldn't find words strong enough to describe my idiocy. If that were only now! If this minute I found a schoolgirl's savings on the street or the last øre of some poor widow, I would jump for it and stick it in my pocket, steal it with calm deliberation, and sleep like a top all night. I hadn't suffered so unspeakably for nothing, my patience was finished, I was ready for anything that came along.

I walked around the castle three or four times, decided

107

to start home, took a couple more swings through the park, and walked finally down Karl Johan Street.

It was about eleven. The street was rather dark, people were wandering about all over, silent couples and noisy groups mingled. The great hour had begun, the mating time when the secret exchanges took place and the joyful adventures began. Rustling petticoats, one or two quick sensual laughs, swelling breasts, rapid heavy breathing; down by the Grand Hotel a voice called, "Emma!" The whole street was a warm swamp, with mists rising from it.

I unconsciously checked my pockets for two kroner. The sexual energy visible in all the gestures of those going by, even in the dim flame of the gas lamps, and the motionless steamy night had all begun to affect me—this air filled with whispers, embraces, hesitant confessions, half-pronounced words, tiny squeals. Even the cats were making love with high-pitched shrieks in the door of Blomqvist's Café. And I didn't have two kroner. What a misery, unheard of, to be this broke! What a disgrace, what a humiliation! I started thinking again about the last mite of some poor widow which I wanted to steal, some schoolboy's cap or handkerchief, some beggar's sack which I would have taken instantly to a rag merchant and drunk up. To console myself, and give myself a little shield, I took to finding every possible fault with the happy people going by me: I shrugged my shoulders in disgust and looked contemptuously after them as they went by, couple after couple. These babyish, aimless, candy-eating students who think they are really being rakish and Continental every time they manage to pat a girl on the breast! These bachelors, bank clerks, butchers, philanderers who don't even draw the line at sailors' wives, or those fat sows from the cattle market who flop down in the nearest doorway for a glass of beer! What Helens! The place beside them still warm from some night watchman or horse hostler of the night before: the throne was always empty, always open, don't hesitate, step right up! . . . I gave a long spit over the sidewalk without bothering about whom it might hit, became furious, full of contempt for these people rubbing against each other and pairing off right before my eyes. I raised my face and felt how blessed I was at being able to keep my path clean.

By the Senate House I met a girl who looked straight at me as we passed.

"Good evening!" I said.

"Good evening!" She stopped.

Hmm. Was she out walking so late? Wasn't it a little dangerous for a young woman to be out on Karl Johan this time of night? No? But hadn't she ever been addressed, molested, I mean hadn't anyone just asked her outright to come home with him?

She looked at me surprised, examined my face to see what I was really saying. Then she suddenly put her hand in under my arm, and said, "All right, let's go then!"

I walked with her. When we were a few steps past the taxi stand, I stopped, freed my arm, and said, "Listen, my dear, I don't have a single øre." And made as if to go my way.

At first she refused to believe me, but after she had felt in all my pockets and found nothing, she got angry, tossed her head, and called me a dried-out stick.

"Good night!" I said.

"Wait a minute," she said. "Aren't those gold rims on your glasses?"

"No."

"All right, go to hell then!"

I walked off.

A few seconds later she came running after me and called to me again.

"You can come home with me anyway," she said.

I felt humiliated by this free offer from a pitiful street whore, and said so. Besides, it was getting late and I had to be somewhere; she really couldn't afford sacrifices of that kind, anyway.

"Now I really *want* you to come."

"But I won't go under these circumstances."

"You're on your way to some other girl," she said.

"No," I answered.

The truth was there wasn't much spring left in me these days. Women had become to me almost like men. Hunger and misery had dried me up. I felt, nevertheless, my embarrassing position in relation to this unusual whore, and I determined to save face.

"What is your name?" I asked. "Marie? So! Now, Marie, listen to me." And I started to explain my behavior. The girl grew more and more astonished. Did she really believe then that I was one of those types who run around the streets at night chasing young girls? Did she really think something that bad about me? Had I ever said anything improper to her up to now? Did people who had evil ideas in mind behave as I did? The fact was I had addressed her and walked a few steps with her just to see how far she would allow it to go. My name, by the way, was such and such, Pastor such and such. Good night! Go and sin no more!

With that I left.

I rubbed my hands, delighted, over my fine story, and talked aloud to myself. What a joy it was to go around doing good deeds! I had maybe given that fallen creature just the shove she needed toward an upright behavior for the rest of her life! And she would be grateful when she thought back on it, maybe even remember me on her deathbed with thanksgiving. Oh, it still paid to be honorable, honorable and righteous! My spirits were high as could be, I felt strong and ready for anything. If I only had a candle, I could finish my article! I walked along, jingling my new doorkey in my hand, hummed, whistled, and debated about how to get a candle. There was nothing else to do, I would have to take my writing stuff downstairs, out under the street lamp. I unlocked the street door and walked up to get my papers.

When I came back down, I locked the street door from the outside and took up my place under the street lamp. Everything was quiet, I heard only the heavy clanking sound of a policeman's footsteps down in Tvær Street, and far away, in the direction of St. Hanshaugen, dogs barking. There was nothing to disturb me, I pulled my coat collar up around my eyes and started thinking as hard as I could. It would be a tremendous help if I were only lucky enough to get the last part of this essay right. I was at a difficult point just now, I needed an imperceptible transition to the next thing, and after that a smooth, gradual finale, a long calm passage which would finally end in a climax as abrupt and shocking as a shot or the sound of a mountain breaking apart. End.

The words would not come. I read the whole piece over from the beginning, read every sentence aloud, and I could not marshal my ideas for this spectacular climax. While I stood there working, who should come but a policeman; he took up a position in the middle of the street a little way off, and ruined my mood completely. What was it to him if I stood here for a moment writing a marvelous climax to an essay for the Chief? God, it was absolutely impossible for me to keep my head above water, no matter what I did! I stood there an hour. The policeman went his way. It got to be too cold for standing still. Discouraged and depressed over this new try come to nothing, I finally opened the street door and went in.

My room was cold, and the darkness so deep I could hardly see the window. I felt my way over to the bed, pulled off my shoes, and set about warming my feet between my hands. At last I lay down to sleep—fully dressed, as I had been doing for a long time.

In the morning I sat up in bed as soon as it was light, and started work on my article again. I sat there without moving until noon; by then I had worked out ten or twenty lines. And I still had not gotten to the finale.

I got up, pulled on my shoes, and started walking back and forth in the room to warm up. Frost was on the windows; I looked out, it was snowing; in the courtyard a thick blanket of snow was lying on the cobblestones and the pump.

I fussed around in my room, walked mechanically back and forth, scraped on the walls with my fingernails, rested my forehead carefully against the door, tapped on the floor with my forefinger, and listened attentively; I was listening for nothing but I listened quietly and thoughtfully as if I were engaged on a matter of considerable importance. All this time I said aloud, over and over, so even I heard it: But God in heaven, this is insanity! I kept on anyway, just as crazily. After a long while, perhaps a couple of hours, I pulled myself together by force, bit my lips, and took hold as best I could. This had to come to a stop! I found a sliver to chew on and sat down, determined to write some more.

A couple of short sentences came into existence with considerable effort, a few miserable words I tortured into being just to make some headway. Then I stopped, my head was empty, I couldn't do any more. When it was obvious that I couldn't go on, I began staring with eyes wide open at these final words, at this unfinished page, gaped at the curious shaky letters which gazed up at me from the paper like small shaggy beings, and at the end I couldn't understand what was going on, I had no thoughts at all.

Time passed. I heard traffic noise outdoors. Noise from wagons and horses, Jens Olai's voice floated up to me from the stable where he was talking to the horses. I was in a real stupor. I smacked my lips once or twice but undertook nothing else. My chest was giving me pain.

Dusk began to fall, I sank into myself more and more, grew tired and lay back on the bed. To warm my hands a bit, I pushed my fingers through my hair, back and forth, crossways and sideways; small handfuls came loose, tufts came away between my fingers and spread over the pillow. I didn't worry about that, it was as if it were not happening to me; I had plenty of hair anyway. After a while I attempted to rouse myself from this curious drowsiness which had floated into all my limbs like a fog; I sat up, coughed as hard as my chest would allow— and fell back once more. Nothing to do, I was dying with open eyes, helpless, staring up at the ceiling. Finally I put my forefinger in my mouth and started sucking on it. Something started to flicker in my brain, an idea that had gotten free in there, a lunatic notion. Suppose I took a bite? Without a moment's hesitation I shut my eyes and clamped down hard with my teeth.

I leaped up. Finally I was awake. A little blood trickled

from the finger, and I licked it off. There wasn't much pain, the wound didn't amount to anything, but I was suddenly myself again. I shook my head, walked to the window, and found a rag for my finger. While I stood puttering about with that, my eyes suddenly filled, I cried softly to myself. The poor bitten thin finger looked so pitiful. My God, I was a long way down.

It got darker—perhaps it would be possible for me to write the finale tonight if I only had a candle. My brain was clear once more. Thoughts came and went as usual, and I wasn't suffering so horribly; hunger wasn't bothering me as much as it did several hours ago, I could certainly hold out till the next day. Maybe I could get a candle on credit if I went to the grocery store and simply explained the situation. I was well known there—in the good days when I still had money I had bought many a loaf in their shop. There was no doubt whatever that I could get a candle on the strength of my good name. So for the first time in weeks I brushed up my clothes a bit and whisked away the loose hairs on my coat collar as well as I could in the dark. Then I felt my way down the stairs.

When I got out on the street, it occurred to me that perhaps I ought to ask for some bread instead. I became indecisive, stopped and thought for a while. "No, absolutely not!" I finally replied to myself. I was unfortunately not in condition now to tolerate food—it would be the same story as before: visions and "feelings" and crazy ideas. My article would never get finished that way, and it was important I visit the Chief soon before he forgot who I was. Absolutely not! I decided definitely on a candle. I walked into the grocery store.

A woman stood at the counter, making purchases; at my side, a number of small parcels were lying, wrapped in various sorts of paper. The clerk, who recognized me and knew what I usually bought, left the woman for a moment, wrapped a loaf of bread quickly in newspaper, and laid it in front of me.

"No—actually it is a candle I need tonight," I said. I

said it very softly and humbly so as not to irritate him and so spoil my chance for the candle.

He hadn't expected that answer; it was the first time I had ever asked for anything besides bread from him.

"All right, you'll have to wait a bit then," he said, and returned to the woman's order.

She received her articles and paid, giving him a five-kroner bill, took the change back from it, and left.

The clerk and I were now alone.

He said, "Oh, yes, it was a candle." He tore open a package of candles and handed one to me.

He looked at me and I looked at him; I couldn't get my request out.

"Oh yes, that's right, you paid," he said suddenly. He said flatly that I had paid: I heard every word. He began pulling up silver coins from the till, krone after krone, shiny, fat coins—he gave me back change for a five-kroner bill, the woman's bill.

"There you are!" he said.

I stood there gaping at the money a second, I was aware that something was wrong somewhere, but I didn't go into it, I thought of nothing at all; I was dazed at the treasure that lay there glittering before my eyes. I gathered the coins up mechanically.

I remained standing by the counter, dumb with amazement, defeated, humiliated; I took a step toward the door and stopped again. I fixed my gaze on a certain point on the wall where a training collar with a small bell hung, and underneath it, a package of shoelaces. I stood gazing at these objects.

The clerk thought I wanted to exchange a few words since I was taking so much time in going, and he said, while tidying up some wrapping paper that was loose on the counter: "It looks as if we're going to have winter now."

"Hmm. Yes," I answered. "It looks as if we're going to have winter now. It looks that way." A second later I added, "Well, it's about time, I think. But it certainly does look that way. Of course it's about time, too."

I heard myself speaking this gibberish but took in each word I spoke as if it were coming from another person.

"Oh, do you think so?" said the clerk.

I put my hand with the money into my pocket, turned the knob, and went out; I heard myself say good night, and the clerk answer.

I was a few steps down the street when the shop door was thrown open and the clerk shouted after me. I turned around without a trace of surprise or a twinge of fear; I simply gathered the coins together in my hand and got ready to give them back.

"For you, you forgot your candle," the clerk said.

"Oh, thank you," I answered calmly. "Many thanks!"

I kept on walking down the street, carrying the candle in my hand.

My first rational thought had to do with the money. I went over to a street lamp and counted it, weighed it in my hand and smiled. In any case, this help was magnificent, incredible, I had been wonderfully helped for a long, long time! I put my hand with the money back in my pocket and walked on.

Outside a basement café in Stor Street I stopped, debating coldly and soberly whether I should risk a small lunch immediately. I heard the clatter of plates and knives inside, and the thump of meat being pounded. The temptation was too great, I walked in.

"One roast beef!" I said.

"One roast beef!" the girl shouted through a little opening in the wall.

I sat down at a small table for one, just inside the door, and prepared to wait. It was a bit dark there, I felt fairly well hidden, and I set myself to think. Once in a while the girl looked over at me with a certain curiosity.

My first really dishonorable act was taken, my first theft, compared to which all my earlier pranks were insignificant; my first tiny, huge fall. . . . So be it! Nothing to do about it. Anyway, I still had freedom of action. I could make it up to the clerk at a later date, when the time was right. I didn't have to keep on being dishonorable, but even so I had never promised I would live any more honorably than anyone else, I hadn't signed any contract. . . .

"Do you think my order will be here soon?"

"Yes, right away." The girl opened the little sliding door and looked into the kitchen.

But suppose the thing came to a head one day? Suppose the clerk were to get suspicious, start to think over the business of the bread and the five kroner the woman got change for? It wasn't impossible it would all come to him one day, maybe the next time I went in. Good God, what a mess! . . . I shrugged my shoulders surreptitiously.

"Here we are!" the waitress said in a friendly way, and set the plate of beef down. "But wouldn't you rather go into the next room? It's awfully dark here."

"No, thank you. Let me stay here," I answered. Her friendliness touched me. I paid for the beef immediately and gave her for a tip whatever coins I got hold of in my pocket; when I did, I closed her hand over them. She smiled, and I said as a joke, my eyes wet: "Keep that to buy an estate with. . . . You're very welcome!"

I started eating; gradually I became more and more ravenous and swallowed whole pieces without chewing them. I tore at the meat like a cannibal.

The waitress came to me again.

"Would you like to have something to drink?" she said. And she leaned over me slightly.

I looked at her; she talked very quietly, almost bashfully. She lowered her eyes.

"I was thinking of a glass of beer, or whatever you'd like . . . on me. . . . No cost. . . . If you would like to. . . ."

"No, thank you very much!" I answered. "Not this time. I'll come back another day."

She went back and sat down behind the counter. I could only see her head. A strange person!

When I was finished, I walked straight to the door. I felt nauseated already. The waitress stood up. I was afraid of getting into the light, frightened of showing myself too clearly to this girl who had no idea of my real poverty, so I said a rapid good night, bowed, and left.

The food began to bother me, my stomach felt upset,

and I would not be able to hold the food down very long. I walked along emptying my mouth, in every dark crook I passed, fought against the nausea which was making me hollow all over again, clenched my fists, steeled myself, stamped on the sidewalk, and swallowed again in a rage what was trying to come up—all in vain! I ran at last into a doorway, doubled over, blinded from the tears that sprang from my eyes, and vomited everything.

Now I was bitter; I walked along the street, sobbing. I cursed the cruel gods, whoever they were, who were persecuting me so, sentenced them to hell and eternal damnation and pain for their infamy. There was very little chivalry among the gods, very little chivalry at all, I could tell you that! . . . I went over to a man who was looking into a store window and asked him as fast as I could what in his opinion one ought to feed a man who had been starving for a long time. It was a matter of life and death, I said. The man couldn't keep beef down.

"I've heard that milk is good in those cases, boiled milk," the man answered, utterly astonished. "For whom, if I may ask, are you inquiring?"

"Many thanks!" I said. "Boiled milk is probably a very good idea."

I walked away.

At the first café I came to, I walked in and asked for some boiled milk. I got the milk, drank it down still scorching as it was, swallowed every drop greedily, and walked out. I started home.

Now the curious thing happened again. Outside the street door of my house, leaning against the lamppost and directly in the light, a person was standing whom I could see even from a long way off—it was the woman dressed in black. The same woman who had been there the previous nights. There was no question about it: for the fourth time running, she had appeared at exactly the same spot. She stood there without moving.

I found this so extraordinary that involuntarily I slowed up. In that instant my brain was working well, even though it was rather excited, and my nerves on edge from the last meal. I walked as usual close to her and past her, got almost to the door, and was about to go inside. Then I stopped. I had an impulse suddenly. Without reasoning with myself at all, I turned around and walked over to the woman, looked into her face and said, "Good evening!"

"Good evening!" she answered.

"Pardon me, but are you looking for someone? I have noticed you here before. Could I be of any help, I wonder? Forgive me for intruding."

Well, she didn't know exactly. . . .

"No one is living inside that door except three or four horses and me—actually the building is a stable and a tinsmith shop. You are probably on a wild-goose chase then, though I'm sorry to say it, if you're looking for someone here."

She turned her face to the side and said, "I'm not looking for anyone, I'm just standing here."

Well, only standing there, but standing there night after night merely on a sort of whim! That was a bit odd —the more I thought about it, the more confused I became. So I decided to be bold. I jingled the coins in my pocket a little and asked her outright to come with me and have a glass of wine somewhere. . . . We'll celebrate the coming of winter, he-he. . . . It wouldn't take long. . . . But perhaps she'd rather not?

No, thank you, she thought she'd better not. She couldn't do it. But would I be so kind as to walk with her a little way. It was rather dark, and it was embarrassing sometimes to walk up Karl Johan Street alone at this time of night.

Delighted.

We started off; she walked at my right side. A peculiar, beautiful feeling came over me. The consciousness of being close to a young girl. I walked along looking at her the whole way. The perfume in her hair, the warmth that poured out from her body, the odor of femininity around her, the sweet breath whenever she turned toward me—it all flowed into me, took control of my senses entirely. I could just make out a plump, slightly pale face behind the veil, and full breasts that pushed out her cape. The thought of all that beauty I sensed was there hidden

118

under the cape and the veil made me feel bewildered, and idiotically happy for no sensible reason. I couldn't hold out any longer, I touched her with my hand, ran my fingers over her shoulder, and smiled like a moron. I heard my heart thumping.

"You're a strange one!" I said.

"Really? Why do you think so?"

"Well, in the first place because you have the curious habit of standing outside a horse barn night after night, with no point in it at all, merely on a sort of whim. . . ."

On the other hand, she could have a purpose of sorts; actually she liked to stay up late, she had always been terribly fond of that. Did I like to go to bed before midnight?

"I? If there is anything in the world I really hate, it is going to bed before twelve o'clock at night!"

Oh, is that so! So that's why, you see, she took a walk like this in the evening when nothing else was going on; she lived up on St. Olaf's Place. . . .

"Ylayali!" I cried.

"Beg your pardon?"

"I merely said Ylayali. . . . Well, well, go on!"

She lived up on St. Olaf's Place, it was lonesome at times, with her mama who wasn't much good to talk to because she was so deaf. Was there anything odd then in her liking to be out of the house a little?

"No, not at all!" I answered.

"You seem very sure of that." I could hear by her voice that she was smiling.

Didn't she have a sister?

Yes, she had an elder sister. But how did I know that? She had gone to Hamburg.

Recently?

Yes, five weeks ago. Where did I find out that she had a sister?

I didn't find it out at all, I just asked.

We fell silent. A man passed us, carrying a pair of shoes under his arm. Otherwise, the street was empty as far down as we could see. Over by the Tivoli a long string of colored lights was shining. The snow had stopped. The sky was clear.

"Heavens, aren't you freezing without an overcoat?" she suddenly asked, looking at me.

Should I tell her why I didn't have an overcoat? Be open about my situation right now and frighten her away —just as well now as later. Still, it was sweet to walk here beside her and keep her in ignorance a little while. I lied, and answered, "Oh, no, not at all." So as to change the subject, I asked, "Have you seen the little zoo over at the Tivoli?"

"No," she answered. "Is it something worth seeing?"

What if she decided she wanted to go there? In those bright lights, among all the people! She would be shocked, I would scare her out of the place with my frightful clothes, my skinny face which I hadn't washed in two days, she would even find out that I had no waistcoat. . . .

"No, I don't think so," I said. "There's not much there to see." A couple of simple ideas luckily occurred to me then, which I immediately put to use, odds and ends from my looted brain: "One can't expect much of such a small zoo. And looking at animals in cages doesn't interest me in general. They know that we are standing there looking at them—they sense the hundreds of inquisitive looks, and it has an effect on them. What I prefer are animals who aren't aware of being watched, shy creatures fussing about in their lairs, lying with half-closed eyelids, licking their claws, and thinking. Don't you think so?"

Yes, she thought I was right.

"The animals that have all their terror and original wildness are the ones that are valuable. The stealthy silent steps in the dead of night, the sighs from boughs, the eeriness of pinewoods, cries from the passing birds, the wind, smell of blood, thunder in the sky; in short, the spirit of wild nature that is still inside the wild creature. . . ."

But I was afraid all this was boring her, and the sense of my own immense poverty seized me again, and depressed me. If I had only been halfway decently dressed, I could have given her the pleasure of a walk in the

120

Tivoli! I couldn't understand this woman who evidently enjoyed being escorted all the way up Karl Johan by a half-naked beggar. What in God's name was she thinking of? And why was I walking here, playing roles and smiling idiotically at nothing? Did I have any sensible reason, really, to let myself be lured by this little silken wren into such a long walk? Wouldn't this overtax me? Didn't I feel the cold of death slip right into my heart every time the slightest wind hit us? And wasn't insanity already setting up house in my brain, purely from lack of food for months on end? She was actually keeping me from going home and sipping a little milk, one more spoonful of milk which I maybe could keep down. Why didn't she just turn her back and let me go to hell? . . .

I became confused, my despair pushed me over the edge, and I said, "Actually, you shouldn't be walking with me; I am degrading you in the eyes of other people by my clothes alone. That is the truth now; I really mean it."

She was taken aback. She looked up at me swiftly and said nothing. Finally she said, "Good heavens!" She said nothing more.

"What do you mean by that?" I asked.

"Oh, please, don't talk like that. . . . We haven't far to go now." And she walked a little faster.

We got to University Street, and we could see the lights in St. Olaf's Place already. Now she walked more slowly again.

"At the risk of being indiscreet," I said, "may I ask you your name before we part? And won't you just for an instant lift your veil so I can see you? I would be very grateful."

Pause. We walked on. I waited.

"You have seen me before," she answered.

"Ylayali!" I said again.

"You followed me once for a half a day and almost home. Were you drunk then?" I could hear again that she was smiling.

"Yes," I said. "Yes, unfortunately I was drunk that time."

"That was very bad of you!"

And I admitted contritely that it was very bad of me. We were at the fountain now; we stopped and looked up at all the bright windows at 2 St. Olaf's Place.

"You mustn't come with me any farther," she said. "I enjoyed the evening, thank you!"

I lowered my head and didn't dare say anything. I took off my hat and stood bareheaded. Would she consider letting me take her hand?

"Why don't you ask me to go back with you a little way?" she said jokingly. But she looked down at the toes of her shoes.

"My God," I said, "yes! If you would let me!"

"Yes, but only a little way."

So we turned around.

I was utterly confused now, I didn't know which end was up; this creature had turned all my expectations upside down. I was delighted, wonderfully glad; I felt as if I were about to collapse from joy. She had expressly wanted to walk back with me, it was her idea, not mine. I walked along, keeping my eyes on her, and became more and more frisky, and she encouraged it, drawing me nearer to her with every word. I forgot for a moment my poverty and misery, my whole horrible situation, I felt the warm blood racing through my body just as in the old days while I was still in one piece physically, and I decided to feel my way further with a little trick.

"Actually, it wasn't you I was following that time," I said. "I was following your sister."

"Was it my sister?" she said, and couldn't have been more amazed. She stopped, looked at me, and waited for me to answer. She was asking in dead earnest.

"Yes," I answered. "Hmm. I mean, I was following the younger of the two women who were walking ahead of me."

"The younger? Aaah!" She laughed all at once, a high, full laugh like a child's. "How sly you are! You said that just to get me to take off my veil. I saw through that. Well, you'll have to turn blue in the face from waiting then . . . . . as punishment."

We started laughing and joking, we talked without stopping the whole time, I didn't know what I was saying, I was happy. She told me she had seen me one time earlier, a long time ago, in the theater. I was with three friends and had behaved like a lunatic; no question, I had been drunk that time too, that was naughty.

"Why did you think that?"

"Well, because you laughed all the time."

"So. Yes, yes, I laughed a lot in those days."

"But not now?"

"Oh yes, now too. Being alive is wonderful!"

We were down to Karl Johan.

She said, "This is as far as we go!" So we turned around and walked back up University Street. When we got up to the fountain again, I slowed up, knowing I would not be able to go with her any farther.

"Now you have to turn around," she said, stopping.

"Yes, I have to," I replied.

But a minute later she thought I could certainly come with her to the door. After all, there was nothing wrong with that, was there?

"No," I said.

But as I stood by the door, all my misery drove in on me again. How could a man keep up his courage when he was broken in two like this? Here I stood, before a young woman, dirty, in rags, deformed by hunger, not washed, half naked—enough to make one sink into the earth. I shrank together, unconsciously stooped a little, and said, "Must I never see you again?"

I had no hope of ever getting to meet her again, I was almost longing for a sharp no which would stiffen me up and make me numb.

"You could."

"When?"

"I don't know."

Pause.

"Won't you be kind enough to lift your veil just for a single instant," I said, "so I can see whom I am talking with? Just one minute. I have to see whom I'm talking to."

Pause.

"You can meet me here Tuesday evening," she said. "Would you want to do that?"

"Lord yes, if you'll let me!"

"Eight o'clock."

"Good."

I ran my hand down over her cape, brushing the snow off it just to get a chance to touch her. I felt great pleasure just in being so near her.

"So you mustn't think that I'm a bad girl then," she said. She smiled again.

"No. . . ."

Suddenly, with a resolute motion, she pulled her veil up on her forehead; we stood looking at each other a second. "Ylayali!" I said. She stood on tiptoe, threw her arms around my neck, and kissed me full on the mouth. I could feel her breast rise and fall, she was breathing rapidly.

In an instant she pulled herself away, called good night in a whispering, husky voice, turned and ran up the stairs without another word. . . .

The street door closed.

The next day it showed still more, a heavy wet snow, great blue flakes that fell and turned to slush. The air was raw and cold.

I woke up rather late, my brain strangely confused by all the excitement of the night before, and my heart drunk from that beautiful meeting. In delight I lay awhile awake, imagining that Ylayali was lying beside me: I reached my arms out, embraced myself, and kissed the air. Finally I got up, went out, and bought a fresh glass of milk, and immediately after, some roast beef. I was no longer hungry—but my nerves were still jangled.

I went off to look for some used clothes. It struck me that I could perhaps buy a used waistcoat very cheaply, something to have on under my coat, anything would do. I walked up the stairs to the secondhand store and picked up a waistcoat which I started to examine. While I was fooling with that, an acquaintance came by, nodded and called to me. I left the waistcoat lying there and walked down to him. He was an engineer on his way to his office.

"Come along and have a glass of beer," he said. "Only come right now, I don't have much time. . . . Who was that woman you were walking with last night?"

"Suppose I informed you," I said, jealous merely that he thought of her, "that she is my fiancée?"

"Marvelous!" he said.

"Yes, that was all arranged last night."

I had knocked him down with that, he believed me without qualification. I lied through my teeth to get rid of him. We got our beer, drank it, and left.

"Good morning! . . . By the way," he said suddenly, "I owe you, you know, several kroner, and it is a crime that I haven't paid them back long ago. But I will pay them back first thing."

"Good, thank you," I said. But I knew he would never pay me back.

The beer unfortunately went to my head, I became extremely warm. Thoughts of last night's adventure flooded over me, made me almost delirious. What if she didn't come on Tuesday? What if she had started thinking it over and became suspicious! . . . Suspicious about what? . . . My mind suddenly went off on a tangent, and became obsessed with the matter of the money. I felt appalled at myself, deathly afraid. The theft stood out before me in all its details: I saw the little shop, the counter, my emaciated hand as I picked up the money, and I imagined to myself the police procedure as they came to arrest me. Irons on wrists and ankles—no, only on wrists, perhaps only one wrist; then hearing the clerk filling out forms, the sound of his pen scraping, his glance, his terrible glance: Now, Mr. Tangen: the cell, eternal darkness. . . .

Hmm. I clenched my fists hard to give me courage, walked faster, and got to the main market square. Here I sat down.

No pranks now! How in hell could anyone prove that I had stolen anything? Besides, the clerk himself would never dare report the incident even if he suddenly remembered one day how it had all gone—he would not want to be fired. No fuss, no scenes, if you please!

But the coins felt heavy in my pocket and kept me from being calm. I started scrutinizing my feelings and found that I had been without the slightest doubt happier before, while I was walking around suffering in honor. And Ylayali! Hadn't I also dragged her down too, with my sinful hands! O God, God in heaven! Ylayali!

I was drunk as a coot, I leaped up suddenly and started toward the cake seller near the Elephant Apothecary. I could still save myself from dishonor, it was not too late, far from it, I would show the whole world what I was capable of! On the way I got the money ready, got every øre into my fist. I bent over the woman's cake board as if I wanted to buy something and suddenly put the money into her hand. I didn't say a word, I turned and left instantly.

How wonderful it felt to be an honorable man again! My empty pockets no longer weighed me down, it was a delight to me to be broke again. Examining it truly, these coins had actually cost me many a secret groan, I had thought of them again and again with shudders. I was not a hardened and damned soul, my honorable nature had risen against that sordid deed, yes it had. Thanks to God, I had raised myself in my own estimation. "Go thou and do as I have done!" I said, looking out over the crowded marketplace, simply do as I have done. I had given a paradise of joy to a poor old woman—she didn't know right now if she was coming or going. Her children would not be climbing into bed hungry tonight. . . . I got myself all worked up with these thoughts and was sure my behavior had been really excellent. Thank God, the money was now out of my hands.

Both excited and drunk, I walked along the street, ready to do great deeds. My joy over being able to come pure and honorable to my meeting with Ylayali, and look her straight in the face, ran away with me, being half drunk anyway. I had no more pains, my head was clear and empty, it felt like a head of pure light which balanced there shining on my shoulders. I felt an urge to pull off

126

practical jokes, to do astounding things, turn the town upside down, and roar. All the way along Grænsen Street I acted like a lunatic; I heard a faint ringing in my ears, and in my brain the alcohol was going full blast. Pushed on by foolhardiness, I got the idea of going up to a city messenger—one who had not said a word to me—and telling him my age; then I would take his hands, look him intensely in the face, and leave again without a word of explanation. I could distinguish the nuances in voices of passers-by, and in their laughter; I made note of several small birds hopping in front of me on the street, and fell to studying the expressions on the cobblestones, in which I found all sorts of omens and wonderful signs. While still at work with this, I came to the square by the Senate House.

Abruptly I stopped and stared at the row of carriages for hire. The drivers were walking around talking with each other, the horses stood bent forward against the snow. "Come along!" I said, giving myself a nudge in the ribs. I walked quickly over to the first carriage and climbed in. "Ullevaals Street, number 37!" I shouted. We rolled away.

As we drove along, the driver began to look behind and bent his head to peep into the carriage where I was sitting under the oilskin hood. Had he become suspicious? There was no question but that my miserable clothes were making him have second thoughts.

"I've got to meet this man," I shouted, forestalling his question, and I explained to him urgently that I absolutely had to meet this man.

We stopped outside number 37, I hopped out, ran up the stairs all the way to the third floor, found a bell knob and pulled. The bells inside gave six or seven frightful clangs.

A girl came and unlocked the door; I noticed that she was wearing gold-drop earrings and black cloth buttons on her bodice. She looked at me, frightened.

"I am looking for Kierulf, Joachim Kierulf, he is a wool buyer, if I might add that, not the sort of man you'd ever forget . . ."

The girl shook her head.

"No Kierulf living here," she said.

She stared at me and took hold of the door, ready to close it again. She made no effort to help—she looked actually as if she knew the person I was asking for, if she would only make the effort, the lazy thing. I got angry, turned my back on her, and ran back down the stairs. "He wasn't there!" I cried to the driver.

"He wasn't there?"

"No. Drive to Tomte Street, number 11."

I was in a wild state of mind and communicated something of that to the driver; he was convinced it was a matter of life and death and drove off without a word. He used his whip on the horses.

"What is the man's name?" he asked, turning on his seat.

"Kierulf, the wool buyer, Kierulf."

The driver agreed that no one could make a mistake about this man. Didn't he usually wear a light-colored coat?

"What was that?" I shouted. "Light-colored coat? Are you out of your mind? What do you think I'm looking for, a teacup?" This light-colored coat displeased me and spoiled my image of the man.

"What was the name you said—Kierulf?"

"Yes, that's it," I said. "Is there anything wrong with that? That name is no disgrace."

"Doesn't he have red hair?"

It was very likely that he did have red hair, and as soon as the driver mentioned it, I was certain he was right. I felt grateful to the poor old driver and told him that he had hit the thing right on the nose—the man was exactly as he said he was. As a matter of fact, I said, it would be an extremely rare thing if a man like that did *not* have red hair.

"I've had him in my cab then several times," the driver said. "He had a knobby stick with him too."

This made the man stand out vividly to me, and I said, "Ha, yes, the truth is, no one has *ever* seen this man *without* that knobby stick in his hand! You can be positive of that, absolutely positive."

"Yes, there was no question, it was the same man that he had driven before. He recognized him. . . .

We drove so that the horse's shoes threw sparks.

Even in my highly worked-up state, I never lost for a moment my presence of mind. We drove past a policeman, and I took note that his badge was number 69. This figure struck me as gruesomely exact, in an instant it was driven like a sliver into my brain. 69, precisely 69, I would never forget that!

I leaned back in the carriage, a prey to the maddest impulses, crept down under the oilskin hood so that no one would see me moving my mouth, and let myself go, chattering idiotically with myself. Insanity flooded through my brain again and I let it come, fully aware throughout of being under the influence of powers I could not control. I started to laugh, silently and passionately, for no reason whatever, still giddy and drunk from the two glasses of beer I had had. Shortly afterwards, my brilliant excitement started to fade, I became more and more calm. My sore finger felt cold, and I put it between my neck and collar to warm it a little. Finally we came to Tomte Street. The cab stopped.

I climbed out slowly, absent-mindedly, depressed, my head heavy. I walked in through the street door, found a courtyard, which I crossed, then I pushed against a door, which opened. I went through and found myself in a hallway, a sort of anteroom, with two windows. Two chests stood, one on top of the other, in a corner, and against the long wall an old painted settee with a rug spread over the seat. To the right, in the next room, I could hear voices and cries of children, and over me in the second story the sound of someone hammering on an iron plate. I took all this in as soon as I entered.

I walked calmly through the room, to the door in the opposite wall, without hurry or thought of escape, opened it also, and found myself in Vognmands Street. I looked up over the door of the house I had just left, and read: *Food and Lodging for Travelers.*

I had not walked through the house in order to escape from the driver who was waiting for me. I walked very soberly along Vognmands Street with no fear and no sense of having done anything wrong. Kierulf, this wool buyer who had been haunting my brain, this person whom I felt positive existed, whom it was essential I find, was gone from my consciousness, whisked away together with other mad notions that came and went in turn. I recalled him now only as a faint sensation, a memory.

I sobered up more and more as I walked, felt fatigued and listless, and pulled my feet along. Snow was still falling in huge wet flakes. Finally I ended up on Grønland Street, near the church, where I sat on a bench to rest awhile. Everyone walking by looked at me in astonishment. I was thinking.

My good God, what a situation I am in now! I was so deeply sick and tired of my whole miserable life that it wasn't worth fighting any longer to keep it. Circumstances had won, they had been too harsh. I was completely worn down, just a shadow of my old self. My shoulders had a serious slump in them from favoring my one side, and I had gotten the habit of leaning over when I walked in order to spare my chest a little. I had examined my body a couple of days ago, one noon up in my room, and I cried the whole time over it. I had worn the same shirt for many weeks now, it was stiff from old sweat, and it had rubbed the point of my navel raw. A little bloody water came out of the wound; even though there was no pain, it was pitiful to have this sore place in the middle of my stomach. There was nothing to do about it, and it wouldn't heal by itself this way; I had washed it, dried it carefully, and put the same shirt on again. Nothing else to do. . . .

I sat on the bench thinking all this over, feeling sad; I was disgusted at myself; even my hands looked revolting to me. The flabby and shameless expression on the back of my hands pained me, brought me disgust. Looking at my emaciated fingers, I felt a nausea move in me, I hated my whole sagging body, and I shuddered having to carry it, to feel it around me. God, if the whole thing would only end now! I sincerely wanted to die.

Completely defeated, lowered in my own estimation,

sullied, I got up mechanically and started to walk home. On the way I passed a house on which I saw these words engraved: "Shrouds available, Miss Andersen, Main Entrance, to the right." "Old memories!" I said, remembering my earlier room on Hammersborg Street, the tiny rocking chair, the newsprint wallpaper down by the door, the Chief of Lighthouses' announcement, Fabian Olsen the Baker's freshly baked bread. Yes, I was so much better off in those days than now—one night I had written a piece worth ten kroner, now I couldn't write anything any more. I could not write a single thing now, my head became instantly empty as soon as I tried. It was time to end the whole business now! I kept on walking.

As I got nearer and nearer to the grocery store, I had the vague sense of approaching danger, but I held firm to my resolve: I was going to turn myself in. I walked calmly up the steps, meeting in the door a small girl who had a cup in her hand: I let her go past and closed the door. The clerk and I once more stood face to face alone.

"Well," he said, "it's dreadful weather."

What was he leading up to? Why didn't he just grab me at once? I became angry and said, "I did not come here to chatter about the weather."

The violence of it flabbergasted him. His little grocer-brain misfired; it had never really occurred to him that I had cheated him of five kroner.

"Don't you know that I robbed you?" I said impatiently, breathing heavily, shivering, and all set to use force if he refused to come to the point instantly.

But the poor creature had no idea of anything.

God in heaven, what stupid people one has to live with! I scolded him firmly, explained to him point by point exactly how it had all taken place, acted out for him where I stood and where he stood when he was giving change, where the money lay, how I had gathered it up in my hand and closed my fist around it—he understood it now, but he still took no action. He turned his head this way and that, listened for footsteps in the next room,

131

put his finger to his lips to get me to talk lower, and at the end said, "That was not a pretty thing to do!"

"No, no, wait a minute!" I cried, feeling a desperate need to contradict him and egg him on. It wasn't really as low and shoddy as he thought with his miserable grocer-brain. I did not *keep* the money, of course, that had never occurred to me. I had wanted no good whatever out of it for myself, my honorable temperament would never have allowed that. . . .

"What did you do with it?"

I gave it away to an old and poor woman, every øre, if he wanted to know; that was the sort of person I was, I never forgot the poor, no matter. . . .

He stood thinking this over a little and became obviously very unsure whether I was an honest man or not. Finally he said, "Don't you think you should have returned the money instead?"

"All right, listen now," I said, arrogantly. "I didn't want to bring any unpleasantness on you, I wanted to spare you. But that is the thanks one gets for being generous. I've been standing here explaining the whole thing to you, and you feel no more shame than a dog, and don't make a single move to settle what is between us. Therefore I am washing my hands of you. You can go to hell. Goodbye!"

I walked out, slamming the door after me.

But when I was home in my room, in my pitiful hole, soaked through from the wet snow, and my knees shivering from the day's exertions, my arrogant mood vanished, and I collapsed again into depression. I regretted my attack on the poor clerk, wept, grabbed hold of my throat to punish myself for my low trick, and made an enormous racket. The clerk had naturally been in terror of losing his job, had not dared to make a fuss over the five kroner the store had lost. And I had taken advantage of his fear, had tortured him with my loud talking, impaled him with every word I had shouted out. The manager himself was probably sitting in the back room about to come out at any moment and see what was going on.

132

No, there was no limit any longer to the disgusting things I was capable of!

But why then hadn't I been locked up? That would have concluded the whole thing. I had as much as reached my wrists out for the handcuffs. I would not have offered the slightest resistance. On the contrary, I would have helped the officer. Oh, God of heaven and of earth, I would give a whole day of my life for one happy second now! My entire life for a mess of pottage! Hear me this once only! . . .

I went to bed in my wet clothes. I had a dim feeling that I would probably die during the night, and I used my last energy to smooth up my bed a little so it would look decent around me in the morning. I folded my hands and chose a good position.

Suddenly I remembered Ylayali. To think that I had forgotten her all night! Some light penetrated very weakly into my consciousness again, a tiny ray of sunlight, making me ecstatically warm. More sunlight flowed in, a gentle delicate silky light, which brushed so sweetly against me. Then the sun grew stronger and stronger, blazing brilliantly on my temples, piercing with heavy and burning heat into my emaciated brain. At the end a mad open fire blazed up before my eyes, a heaven and an earth ignited, men and animals of fire, mountains of fire, devils of fire, a chaos, a wilderness, a universe on fire, a smoking final day.

I saw and heard no more. . . .

The next morning I woke sweating, my whole body damp—my fever had gone up considerably. In the beginning I wasn't clear in my mind what was happening to me, I looked around me astonished, felt my being had somehow entirely changed, did not recognize myself. I felt over my arms and down over my legs, could not get over the fact the window was on one wall and not on the wall exactly opposite, and I heard the stamping of the horses downstairs as if they came from overhead. I was also rather nauseated.

My hair lay on my forehead wet and cold; I sat up on my elbow and looked down at the pillow: wet hair was also lying there in small tufts. My feet had swollen during the night inside my shoes; there was no pain, but I could barely move my toes.

Toward late afternoon, when it was already beginning to be dusk, I got up and started puttering about the room. I tried walking with short, deliberate steps, careful to keep my balance and spare my feet as much as I could. I was not really suffering, and I didn't cry; on the whole I wasn't even sad; I was on the contrary wonderfully at peace—the thought that anything could be any different than it was never once crossed my mind.

Finally I went out.

Only my hunger bothered me, and I felt it despite my nausea. I began to notice a shameless appetite again, a ravenous desire for food inside that grew steadily worse and worse. It gnawed without mercy in my chest, kept up a strange and silent labor in there. It was like a couple of dozen tiny creatures who put their heads over to one side and gnawed awhile, then put their heads over to the other side and gnawed awhile, lay for a moment absolutely still, started again, bored their way in without making noise or hurrying, and left behind them empty areas wherever they went. . . .

I wasn't sick, merely weak, and I started sweating again. I decided to go to the marketplace and rest there, but it was a long, tiresome walk. When I was nearly there, I stopped at the corner of Torvet Street and the marketplace. Sweat ran down in my eyes, clouded my glasses, and made me blind—I stopped to dry myself off a bit. I paid no attention to where I was standing, I didn't worry about it: the noise around me was terrific.

Suddenly I heard a cry, a cold sharp "Look out!" I heard the shout, heard it very well, and I gave a start to the side, took a step as quickly as my feeble legs would allow. A monster of a bread cart shot past me, brushing my coat with its wheel; if I had been a little quicker I would have gotten by scot-free. I could have moved a bit faster, a tiny bit faster, if I had strained myself—but there was nothing to do about it now, one foot hurt, a couple of toes had been crushed. It felt as if they had just curled up, so to speak, inside my shoe.

The driver pulled in the horses with all his might; he turned on his seat and asked in a frightened voice how I was. Oh, it could have been much worse . . . it probably wasn't so bad . . . I didn't think there was anything broken . . . I hoped not. . . .

I limped over to a bench as fast as I could; all the people who had stopped, and were now staring at me, made me self-conscious. It actually wasn't any fatal blow, I had even been lucky, considering that some catastrophe was clearly looking for me. The worst part was that my shoe had been split open; the sole was torn loose from the top. I held my foot up and saw blood in the gap. Well, this was not done intentionally by either of the parties, the driver was certainly not trying to make things worse for me than they were; he looked extremely frightened. Maybe if I had asked him for a little bread from his van I would have gotten it. He would certainly have given me some gladly. May God pay him back only with blessings, wherever he is!

I was bitterly hungry and didn't know what to do with my exorbitant appetite. I writhed about on the bench, and pulled my knees up against my chest as hard as I could. When it was dark, I shuffled over to the city jail—God knows how I got there—and sat down on the edge of the balustrade. I ripped one of my coat pockets out and started chewing on it, not for any purpose particularly, and in a hopeless mood, my eyes staring straight in front of me without seeing. I heard some small children who were playing around me, and I instinctively became alert whenever someone walked past me; otherwise, I was oblivious to the world.

All at once I got the idea of walking down to one of the open-air booths underneath and getting a piece of raw meat. I stood up, crossed the balustrade, over toward the far end of the booths, and walked down the stairs. When I was nearly down to the butcher stalls, I shouted up through the stair arch and motioned angrily backwards as if talking to a dog up there, and then spoke boldly to the first butcher I met.

"Would you be so good as to give me a bone for my dog?" I said. "Just a bone—it doesn't have to have any meat on it, just something he can carry around in his mouth."

I got a bone, a gorgeous little bone with some meat still on it, and put it under my coat. I thanked the man so warmly that he looked at me astonished.

"Nothing to thank me for," he said.

"Oh yes, there is," I said. "This was very good of you."

I walked back up. My heart thumped inside.

I sneaked into a blacksmith's yard, as far in as I could go, and stopped in front of a fallen-down gate in the back. There was not a light visible anywhere, the darkness was sweet and thick all around me; I started chewing on my bone.

It had no taste at all; a nauseating odor of dried blood rose from the bone, and I started throwing up immediately, I couldn't help it. I tried again—if I could only keep it down, it would do some good; the problem was to get it to stay down there. But I vomited again. I grew angry, bit fiercely into the meat, ripped off a small piece, and swallowed it by force. That did no good either—as soon as the small pieces became warm in the stomach, up they came again. I clenched my fists madly, started crying from sheer helplessness, and gnawed like a man possessed, I cried so much that the bone became wet and messy with tears. I vomited, swore, and chewed again, cried as if my heart would break, and threw up again. Then I swore aloud and consigned all the powers of the universe to hell.

Silence. Not a person around, no lights, not a sound. I was in a wild state, I breathed heavily and audibly, and sobbed, gnashing my teeth, every time I had to abandon these bits of meat which might have satisfied my hunger. When nothing helped, no matter how hard I tried, I threw the bone against the gate, maddened by the most impotent hatred. Carried away by rage, I shouted and roared threats up to the sky, shrieked God's name hoarsely and savagely, and curled my fingers like claws. . . . I'll tell you this, you sacred Baal in the sky, you do not exist, and if you do, I'll curse you so that your heaven will start shuddering with hellfire! I'm telling you this, you know I offered myself as your servant, and you rejected me, you pushed me away, and now I turn my back on you for all eternity because you did not know your time of visitation! I'm telling you this, I know that I am going to die, and I mock you anyway, even face to face with death, you Apis in the sky! You have used force against me and you don't realize that force does not work with me. Couldn't you have seen that? Were you asleep when you made my heart and my soul? I am telling you this, all my energy and every drop of blood in me rejoices that I mock you and spit on your grace. From this hour on, I will renounce all your works and all your ways, I will exile my thoughts if they think of you again, and I will rip my lips out if they say your name once more. Now if you do exist, I will tell you my final word in life or in death, I tell you goodbye. And so I am dumb, and I turn my back on you, and I go my way. . . .

Silence.

I was trembling from excitement and exhaustion, and kept on standing in the same spot, whispering oaths and epithets, hiccuping after my long crying spell, fatigued and sluggish after my lunatic outburst of rage. Hell! All I was capable of, even deep in misery, was rhetoric and belles-lettres, it was all talk. I stood there maybe a half hour, hiccuping and whispering and holding on to the gate. Finally I heard voices, a conversation between two men who were coming into the yard. I slunk away from my spot, pulled myself along by holding on to the sides of houses, and came out into the lit streets. While I staggered on down Youngsbakken Street, my brain suddenly started off in a most peculiar direction. It struck me that the old shacks in the corner of the marketplace, the lean-tos holding miscellaneous stuff, and the ancient stalls with secondhand clothes were really a disgrace to the town. They destroyed the view in the market, ruined the city, ugh, tear the whole mess down! I walked along, turning over in my mind what the cost would likely be to move the Geographical Society Building, whose lovely lines always pleased me whenever I passed it, down there. Probably a moving job of that sort couldn't be done for less than seventy to seventy-two thousand kroner—a nice sum, one might say, a tidy little sum as spending money, to start with anyway. And I nodded my empty head, and agreed that it would be a tidy enough sum for spending money, to start with. My whole body was shivering, and I hiccuped deeply now and then after my long cry.

I had the sensation that there wasn't much life left in me, that I was singing the last verse. It was all one to me; my imminent death didn't bother me in the slightest—on the contrary, I went wandering on through the town, down to the wharfs, farther and farther from my room. For that matter, I could very easily have lain right down in the street and died. My pains were making me more and more callous: I felt a throbbing in my sore foot, I even had the impression the pain was moving up my whole leg; the pain, however, was never really unbearable. I had lived through worse sensations.

I arrived finally at the railway pier. There was no traffic, no noise; once in a while a person could be seen, a longshoreman or a sailor, strolling around with his hands in his pockets. I noticed a lame man who looked sharply at me as we passed. Without pausing a second, I stopped him, raised my hand to my hat, and asked whether *The Nun* had sailed yet. When I had finished saying that, I couldn't stop myself from snapping my fingers once right in his face, and saying, "Yes, by God, *The Nun!*" I had entirely forgotten *The Nun*. The thought of it must have been sleeping somewhere far inside, I was carrying it around without being aware of it myself.

"Oh hell yes, *The Nun* is gone."

Could he possibly tell me where it had sailed to?

The man thought awhile, standing on his longer leg and holding the shorter one in the air; the shorter one hung there faintly swinging.

"No," he said. "Do you know what it took on here?"

"No," I answered.

But I had already forgotten *The Nun* anyway, and I

asked the man how far it was to Holmestrand, measured in good old geographical miles.

"To Holmestrand? I would guess . . ."

"Or to Veblungsnæs?"

"What I was about to say, I would guess to Holmestrand . . ."

"Never mind, suddenly I remember it," I interrupted him again. "You wouldn't be so good as to give me a little smidgen of tobacco, just a tiny bit!"

I got the tobacco, thanked him warmly, and walked off. I didn't make use of the tobacco, just stuck it in my pocket. The man did not take his eyes off me, possibly I had awakened suspicion in some way or other. Pausing or walking, I felt that suspicious stare on me, and I didn't feel like being followed by this character. I turned around and went back to him, looked at him and said, "Welt binder."

Just that: "Welt binder." Nothing else. I looked very sternly at him as I said it, I felt I was giving him a fierce and terrible stare—it was as if I were looking at him from another world. I stood there a moment after I spoke that word. Then I plodded up toward the market square by the railway station again. The man did not utter a sound, he just kept his eyes on me.

"Welt binder?" I stopped suddenly. The truth was exactly as I had sensed it the first instant: I had met this cripple before. Up on Grænsen Street one sunny morning: I had pawned my waistcoat then. It seemed like an eternity since that day.

While I stood thinking about this—I was standing leaning against a house at the corner of Torvet and Havne Street—I suddenly gave a start and felt a longing to creep away on my hands and knees. At last I just stared ahead in dismay, and swallowed my shame, there was nothing to do about it—I was face to face with the Chief. I became shameless and took a step out from the house wall to make sure he would notice me. I did that not to awaken pity but simply to humiliate myself, to put myself in the stocks. I could easily have flopped down in the street also and

139

invited the Chief to walk over me, step on my face. I didn't even say good evening to him.

The Chief seemed to sense that I was trying to make some signal; he slowed up a little, and I said, in order to stop him: "I should have brought something to you, but it is still not finished."

"Oh?" he answered, questioning. "You haven't got it ready yet?"

"No, I haven't got it ready."

But now tears suddenly came into my eyes because of his friendliness, and I coughed and cleared my throat sharply to stiffen myself up. The Chief brushed his nose with his thumb; he stood looking at me.

"Do you have anything to live on meanwhile?" he said.

"No," I answered, "I don't. I haven't eaten anything yet today, but . . ."

"God help us, man, that won't do—you can't walk around starving to death!" he said. And he reached at the same time for his wallet.

Now I began to feel shame, I lurched over to the house wall again, and held on to it. I stood watching the Chief poke about in his wallet, but I said nothing. He handed me a ten-kroner bill. He didn't make any fuss about it, he just gave me ten kroner. At the same time he repeated that it wouldn't do for me to starve to death.

I stuttered out an objection and did not take the bill right away. "That was shameful of me to . . . This is much too much. . . ."

"Oh, nonsense," he said, and looked at his watch. "I'm waiting for a train, I think I hear it coming now."

I took the money, was paralyzed with joy, and didn't say another word, I didn't even thank him.

"It's not worth being embarrassed about," the Chief said at last. "Besides, you can always write for it, I know that."

Then he left.

When he was a few steps away, I remembered all at once that I had not thanked him for his help. I tried to catch up to him but couldn't go fast enough, my leg didn't work right and I nearly fell on my face several

140

times. He got farther and farther away. I gave up the chase, thought of shouting after him but didn't dare, and when I finally did decide to do it and called once, then twice, he was already too far off, my voice had grown too weak.

I stood there on the sidewalk looking after him, weeping silently. "I never saw such a thing!" I said to myself. "He gave me ten kroner!" I walked back and stood right where he had stood and acted out all his movements. Then I held the bill up to my wet eyes, inspected it on both sides, and started to swear—swore to high heaven that there was absolutely no question about it: I was holding a ten-kroner bill in my hand.

Sometime later—perhaps considerably later, for the city had become very quiet by this time—I found myself standing, strangely enough, outside 11 Tomte Street. This is where I had cheated a cabbie who had driven me once, and where I had walked straight through the house without having been noticed. I collected myself for a moment and wondered about it all, and then walked in through the door for the second time, right into the *Food and Lodging for Travelers*. Here I inquired about a place to stay and immediately got a room.

Tuesday.

Sunlight, no wind, a wonderfully clear day. The snow was gone; everywhere life and happiness and glad faces, smiles and laughter. The columns of water arched up over the fountains, turned gold from the sunlight and deep blue from the blue sky. . . .

About two in the afternoon I left my room on Tomte Street where I was still living very comfortably on the Chief's ten-kroner note, and went out. I was in the highest spirits and wandered around all afternoon in the busiest streets I could find, looking at people. Even before the clock showed seven in the evening, I made a swing up to St. Olaf's Place and took a furtive look up at the windows of number 2. In one hour I would see her! I walked around in a sweet, delightful anxiety the whole time. What would happen? What would I find to say when she came down the stairs? Good evening? Or should I just smile? I decided to let it go with just a smile. Of course I would bow very very deeply also.

I sneaked off again, a little ashamed of being there so early, strolled along Karl Johan Street awhile, keeping my eye on the university clock. When it was eight, I started up University Street. On the way it occurred to me that I would maybe be a minute or two late, and I pushed on as fast as I could. My foot was rather painful, otherwise I was in good spirits.

I took up my position by the fountain and caught my breath. I stood there quite a while looking at the windows in number 2, but she didn't come. Well, I would wait awhile anyway, I was in no hurry; perhaps something was keeping her. I waited some more. Surely I hadn't dreamed the whole thing? The first meeting—had that been all a fantasy the night I was in bed, feverish? I began to cast about wildly and was not absolutely positive either way.

"Hmmm!" came from behind me.

I heard this slight clearing of the throat, and I heard light steps nearby, but I didn't turn around, I kept on staring at the stairway inside the house.

"Good evening!" I heard then.

I was so astounded to see her coming from that direction that I forgot to smile, I didn't even take off my hat right away.

"Have you been waiting long?" she said, breathing a little rapidly after her walk.

"No, not at all, I just came a moment ago," I answered. "But nothing lost if I had. Do you know, I was positive that you would be coming from the other direction?"

"I walked with Mama to some friends' house—Mama is visiting them tonight."

"I see!" I said.

We had started walking now. A policeman stood on the street corner watching us.

"But where are we going then?" she said, stopping.

"Wherever you want to, wherever you'd like to go."

142

"Oh, having to decide yourself is so boring."

Pause.

Then I said, just to have something to say, "Your windows are dark, I see."

"Yes!" she answered, gaily. "The servant girl is off tonight too. So I am home all alone."

We both stood looking up at the windows of number 2 as if neither of us had ever seen them before.

"Shall we go up to your place then?" I said. "I'll sit quietly by the door, like a mouse, if you want me to. . . ."

But then I shivered and regretted intensely being so bold. What if she became offended and walked away? What if I would never get to see her again? And my miserable clothes! I waited, frightened, for her answer.

"You certainly won't sit down by the door," she said.

We went up.

Out in the corridor, which was dark, she took my hand and led me. I didn't have to be so quiet, she told me, I could certainly talk if I wanted to. We walked in. While she lit a candle—she didn't light a lamp, but a candle— while she lit the candle, she said with a tiny laugh: "You mustn't look at me, ugh, I am ashamed of myself! But I will never do it again."

"What won't you ever do again?"

"I'll never . . . no, such a . . . I'll never kiss you again."

"Oh, really, won't you?" I said, and we both laughed. I reached for her, and she glided to the side, slipped away to the other side of the table. We stood looking at each other a little while, the candle standing between us.

Then she started to take off her veil, and her hat, but all the time she kept her playful eyes on me, watching all my movements so I wouldn't be able to catch her. I made one more try, tripped on the carpet, and fell: my sore foot didn't want to work. I got up extremely embarrassed.

"Good Lord, how you are blushing!" she said. "Do you feel as clumsy as all that?"

"Yes."

Then we started again, running around the table.

"Aren't you limping?"

"I'm limping a little, it doesn't amount to anything."

"The last time you had a sore finger, today you have a sore foot. It's awful, the number of troubles you have!"

"Someone ran over me slightly the other day."

"Ran over? So, drunk again? Your living habits are a disgrace, young man!" She scolded me with her forefinger, and looked grave. "Now we'll sit down!" she said. "No, not over there by the door: you are too shy, over here, you there, and I here, like that. . . . Oh, shy people are such a bore! You, for example, you might have put your hand on the back of my chair, you could certainly have thought that up by yourself, couldn't you? Because if I suggest anything of that sort, you immediately turn two huge saucer eyes at me as if to say you don't really believe your ears. Yes, you do, I've seen it several times already, you are doing it now too. But don't try to get me to believe you are modest like that all the time—I know what you are like. You were awfully fresh that day when you were drunk and followed me nearly home, pestering me with your witticisms: 'You are losing your books, miss, really, honestly, you are losing your book, miss!' Aa-ha-ha! That was frightful of you!"

I sat fascinated looking at her. My heart beat wildly, blood was racing through my veins. What a marvelous sensation to be sitting in a human house again and to hear a clock tick, and to talk with a spirited young girl instead of with myself!

"Why don't you say anything?"

"Oh, what a sweet creature you are!" I said. "I am sitting here in love with you, right now I am your captive entirely. There is nothing to do about it. You are the strangest person. . . . Sometimes your eyes shine so, I've never seen anything like it, they look like flowers. No? No, no, maybe not like flowers, but . . . I am head over heels in love with you, and it won't do me a bit of good. What is your name? You really have to tell me now what your name is. . . ."

"Mine, no, what is your name? Good Lord, here I have nearly gone and forgotten it again! All day yesterday I thought to myself that I must ask you. Well, I can't say *all* day yesterday. I certainly did not think about you *all* day."

"Do you know what my name for you was? I called you Ylayali, what do you think of that? A wonderful, flowing sound. . . ."

"Ylayali?"

"Yes."

"Is that a foreign language?"

"Hmmm. No, no."

"Well, it isn't really ugly."

After long negotiations, we told each other our names. She sat down beside me on the sofa and pushed the chair away with her foot. We started chattering again.

"You've had a shave tonight too," she said. "You look on the whole a little better than you did last time, but only just a teeny bit better—I wouldn't want you to think. . . . No, last time you were really awful. On top of it all, you went around with an old rag on your finger. And in that condition you were absolutely determined to take me in for a glass of wine! No, thank you!"

"Then it was because I looked so bad that you refused to go in with me that time?" I said.

"No," she answered, looking down. "No, God help me, that wasn't it! I didn't even think about that at the time."

"Well," I said, "I'm afraid you're sitting here under the mistaken assumption that I can dress and live exactly as I want to, aren't you? But I can't do it, I am poor, very poor."

She looked at me.

"Is that so?" she said.

"Yes, I'm afraid it is."

Pause.

"Good gracious, I am poor myself," she said, with a bold toss of her head.

Every one of her words made me drunk, went straight to my head like sips of wine, despite the fact that she was more or less the usual kind of Christiania girl, with her slang and daring little sallies and snappy talk. Yet she delighted me with the way she had of letting her head

145

fall a little to one side as she listened to me talk. I felt her breath too, so close to my face.

"Do you know?" I said. "You mustn't be angry now . . . when I was in bed last night I arranged my arm just so . . . like that . . . as if you were lying in it. That is the way I went to sleep."

"Really! That was lovely!" Pause. "Of course there had to be a lot of distance between us before you could do something like that, because if there hadn't been . . ."

"You think that otherwise I wouldn't have done it?"

"That's right, I don't think you would have."

"You should prepare for anything from me," I said, "and everything." I drew myself up and put my arm around her waist.

"Oh, should I do that?" was all she said.

It irritated me that she thought I was too timid and respectable. I threw out my chest, took the leap, and closed my hand over hers. She, however, withdrew it very quietly and moved a little way away. That finished off my courage; I felt ashamed and looked over toward the window. My situation was so humble that I had to be careful not to put on airs. It would have been a different matter altogether if I had met her while I still looked like a man, in my prosperous days when I still had a few reserves. I felt dejected and depressed.

"There you see!" she said. "That's a perfect example. A person can bring you down with just a tiny wrinkle in the forehead, demolish you just by moving away a few inches. . . ." She laughed mischievously, her eyes entirely closed, as if she really couldn't bear to be looked at.

"Oh, you little fox!" I burst out. "All right, you'll see then." And I threw my arms firmly around her shoulders. Girl at a distance, beware! So she took me for an inexperienced boy. By the Lord, she would change her tune. . . . No one should say about me that I couldn't keep up in *this* game. By the living Jesus, if all I had to do was to stay with it . . .

As though there were anything in this world I couldn't do!

She sat quietly all this time, with her eyes still closed:

neither of us spoke; I pressed her hard against me, crushed her body against my chest, and she did not say a word. I could hear our heartbeats, hers and mine, they sounded like horses stamping.

I kissed her.

I didn't know what I was doing any longer, I said some nonsense that she laughed at, mumbled sweet names at her lips, brushed her cheek, kissed her again and again. I opened a button or two in her bodice and glimpsed her breasts, white, swelling breasts that peeked out like two marvels behind her lace.

"I have to see!" I said, and struggled with several more buttons, trying to make the opening larger. But my efforts were too rough, I couldn't make any headway with the last few buttons near her waist which were tight anyway. "But I have to see . . . a little more. . . ."

She threw her arms around my neck, very slowly and tenderly; from her nostrils that were rosy and trembling I could feel her breath right against my face. With one hand she began to undo the buttons herself, one after the other. She laughed self-consciously, a short laugh, looking up at me several times to see if I noticed how frightened she was. She loosened the ties, unhooked the corset over her breasts, was excited and afraid. And I fumbled with my coarse hands among these buttons and hooks. . . .

In order to divert attention, she ran her left hand over my shoulder and said, "You have so many loose hairs lying here!"

"Yes," I said, and tried to press my mouth in toward one of her breasts. At this moment her clothes were entirely open. All at once she seemed to think better of it, she seemed to feel she had gone too far. She pulled her clothes back together and sat up a little. So as to hide her shyness over the unbuttoned clothes, she started talking again about all the fallen hair which lay on the shoulders of my coat.

"What can have made all that hair fall out?"

"Don't know that."

"You drink too much, of course, and maybe even . . . No, I won't even say it! You should be ashamed of yourself! I would never have thought that of you! To think of you so young and already losing your hair! . . . Now, if you please, I want you to describe how you live—what you really do. I'm sure your habits are frightful! But only the truth now, you understand, no covering up! I'll be able to tell anyway when you are trying to hide something. All right, tell me now!"

Oh, how tired I was! I would have been so glad just to sit there quietly looking at her rather than to embark on such labors. I was no good for anything, I was just a block of wood.

"All right, start now!" she said.

I took the opportunity and I told her everything, telling nothing but the truth. I didn't make anything worse than it was, I wasn't trying to make her pity me—I even told her about my stealing five kroner one night.

She sat listening to me with open mouth, pale and frightened, her clear eyes deeply troubled. I tried to repair it again, to lift the gloom that had settled in the room. I straightened up and said, "Oh well, that is all over now! No use talking about that any longer, I'm over the hump now, I'm safe. . . ."

But she was still depressed. "Oh, my God!" was all she said, and then she would be quiet. She would wait a minute and then say it again and once more lapse into silence. "Oh, my God!"

I began to joke, took hold of her to tickle her, lifted her to my chest. She had buttoned her dress again, and that annoyed me. Why should she have buttoned her dress again? Was I of less value in her eyes now than if I had earned my fallen hair by leading a corrupt life? Would she have thought more of me if I had been a roué? . . . No nonsense now! All that was required of me was to follow through— And if that was all that was required, I was just the man for it.

I had to start again.

I pulled her over, simply drew her down on the sofa. She struggled, not very much, and looked at me astonished.

"No . . . what is it?" she said.

"What is it?"

"No . . . no, no . . . ?"

"Yes, yes. . . ."

"No, listen!" she cried. Then she added a wounding sentence. "Sometimes I think you are insane."

I felt checked a little suddenly, and I said, "You don't mean that!"

"Yes, you look so strange! And that morning when you were following me—you weren't drunk then?"

"No. But on the other hand I wasn't starving either— I had just eaten."

"That's even worse then."

"Would you prefer me to have been drunk?"

"Yes . . . oh, I am afraid of you! Oh God, can't you just let me go!"

I thought about that. No, I couldn't let her go, I would lose too much that way. No hanky-panky foolishness this time of the night on a sofa! Good Lord, what excuses women can think up at a time like this! As if I didn't know it was all nothing but bashfulness, modesty! I must be firm, then! Come now, be good! No more nonsense!

She struggled rather hard, too hard to be struggling only from modesty. I knocked the candle over accidentally, so it went out. She made desperate opposition, and even gave out a little whimper.

"No, don't! Don't! You can kiss me on my breast if you want to instead. My sweet thing!"

I stopped instantly. She sounded so dismayed, so helpless, that I felt a blow inside. She was offering me a compensation by giving me permission to kiss her breast! How lovely, how lovely and how naïve! I could have fallen on my knees before her.

"You darling!" I said, utterly confused. "I don't understand this. . . . I don't really grasp which game all this is. . . ."

She got up and lit the candle again with shaking hands. I sat there on the sofa, my mind blank. What would happen now? I was very ill at ease.

She glanced at the wall where the clock was, and gave a start.

"Oh dear, the girl will be home soon!" she said. These were the first words she had said since we sat up.

I understood this hint and stood. She reached for her cape as if to put it on, then thought better of it, let it lie, and walked over to the fireplace. She was pale and became more and more nervous. So that it shouldn't look as if she were just showing me out, I said, "Was your father in the army?" and at the same time I got ready to leave.

"Yes, he was. How did you know that?"

"I didn't know it, it just suddenly occurred to me."

"That was strange!"

"Yes, I suppose. When I come into certain places, I can sense things. That's all part of my insanity. . . ."

She looked up quickly but said nothing. I felt my presence was painful to her, and wanted to make my farewell short. I walked to the door. Would she kiss me again now? Or even let me take her hand? I waited.

"Are you going now?" she said, still standing by the fireplace.

I didn't answer. I felt humbled and bewildered and looked at her without saying anything. God, what I had destroyed! It didn't seem to bother her that I was ready to go; she was lost to me once and for all, and I searched for some way to tell her goodbye, some deep, heavy words that would get through to her and maybe impress her a little. Then I behaved exactly opposite to the way I had intended: I acted wounded instead of being proud and cold; disturbed and insulted, I started to chatter on about trivialities. The tellings words refused to come, I was carrying on like a numbskull. Everything became drivel and rhetoric again.

Why hadn't she just told me simply and clearly to leave? I asked. Well, well, why not? There was no reason to be so polite. Instead of reminding me that the girl would soon be coming back, she could simply have said this: You must leave now, because I must go over and fetch my mother, and I'd rather not have you escort me down the street. Now, wasn't that what she was thinking? Oh yes, that is what she was thinking anyway, I understood it right away. It didn't need much to make me understand—simply the way she reached for her cape and then left it where it was had shown me immediately. As I said, I sensed a lot of things. Perhaps that wasn't really so insane as it seemed. . . .

"Oh my God, forgive me for that word! It just popped out!" she cried. But she stood where she was and still did not come over to me.

I was unrelenting, and went on. I stood there jabbering, all the time with the painful sensation that I was boring her, that not a single one of my words had really penetrated. Nevertheless, I couldn't stop. Actually, in my opinion, a man didn't have to be insane to be sensitive. There were people who could be wounded by trifles and whom a single hard word could kill. I gave her to understand that I was that sort of person. My poverty in fact had actually sharpened some of my faculties and so had increased my sufferings too, that's right, increased my sufferings. Of course that sharpening had its good side as well, it was a help in certain situations. The intelligent poor man of course is a much finer observer than the intelligent rich man. The poor man has to look carefully around him every time he takes a step, he wisely mistrusts every word he hears from others; for him the simplest acts involve obstacles and problems. His senses are sharp, he is a man of feeling, he has experienced painful things, his soul has been burned and scarred. . . .

And I went on a long time about these scars on my soul. But the longer I talked, the more upset she became; finally she blurted out, "Oh my God!" a couple of times in despair, wringing her hands. I could see I was torturing her; I didn't want to torture her, but I kept on doing it anyway. At last I felt most of what needed saying had been said; the look of despair on her face moved me, and I shouted:

"All right, I'm leaving, I'm leaving! Don't you see I already have my hand on the doorknob? Goodbye! I am saying goodbye! You could at least answer me when I say goodbye two times, and am standing here ready to leave. I won't even ask you to let me see you again, because I know that would be painful to you, but I want you to answer me this: Why didn't you let me be? What did I ever do to you? I wasn't really bothering you, was I? And why were you suddenly cold to me as if you didn't know me any more? Now you've taken everything I had left, I'm worse off now than I was before. But so help me God, I'm not insane. You'll realize now if you think about it that there is nothing wrong with me. Come here then and give me your hand! Or let me come over to you! May I do that? I won't do anything bad, I will just kneel in front of you one minute, kneel there on the floor in front of you, just one moment—may I? No, no, all right, I won't do it, I can see you're frightened, I won't, listen, I *won't* do it. But, my God, why are you so terrified? I'm standing still, I'm not moving a muscle. I wanted to kneel on the carpet a moment, right there, on that big red patch by your foot. But you became frightened, I could see instantly in your eyes that you were afraid, so I stood still. I didn't move an inch while I was asking you if I could do it, did I? I was just as motionless then, when I showed you the spot where I wanted to kneel, there on that red rose in the carpet, as I am now. I didn't even point with my finger, I didn't point at all, I let it go so as not to scare you, I just nodded over in that direction, like this! And you understood very well which rose I meant, but you won't allow me to kneel there—you're afraid of me, and you don't dare come near me. I don't understand, though, how you could let yourself call me insane. That is not true, and you don't believe it yourself any longer, do you? One summer, a long time ago, I did go crazy—I was working too hard and I forgot to eat as I should have. My mind was full of ideas. I forgot day after day—I ought to have remembered to eat, but I constantly forgot. So help me God, it is the truth! May God strike me down right here if I am lying! There, you can see, you are being unjust with me. And I didn't do it from having no money —I had credit, my credit was excellent, at both Ingebret's Grocery and Gravesen's. I often had a lot of money in my pockets, and yet I never bought food—simply because I forgot to. It's really the truth! You don't say anything, you never answer, you never leave your spot at the fire-place, you're just waiting for me to go. . . ."

She came swiftly to me and reached out her hand. I looked very mistrustfully at her. Was she really doing that spontaneously! Or was she doing it just to get rid of me? She put her arms around my neck, there were tears in her eyes. I just stood looking at her. She reached up her lips to me; I couldn't believe her, this was only a sacrifice, a way to get it all over with.

She said something which sounded to me like "I love you anyway!" She said it so softly and inaudibly that per-haps I didn't hear quite right, maybe she didn't say exactly those words, but she threw her arms passionately around my neck, she kept both arms around my neck, even raised herself on tiptoe to be taller and remained on tiptoe a little while.

I was afraid she had forced herself to show me this affection, and all I said was "How beautiful you are now!"

That was all I said. I stepped back, bumped the door with my shoulder, and walked out backwards. And she stayed where she was.

PART FOUR

WINTER had come, a raw wet winter almost without snow, a foggy and dark night that went on forever; for a whole week there would be no break in the fog. The street lamps burned almost all day, and people bumped each other anyway in the fog. The city sounds, the chimes from the church steeples, harness bells on the horses, voices of people, hoof clatter, all came through the thick air sounding muffled and underground. Week after week went by and the weather remained exactly the same.

I still had my room in the Vaterland district.

I became more and more attached to this *Food and Lodging for Travelers;* I was still living there even though I was now broke again. My money had long since been used up, but I continued to come and go in the house as if I had some right to it and belonged there. The landlady had not said a word so far, but my not being able to pay her worried me. Three weeks went by this way.

For several days now I had been writing again, but I wasn't able to do anything that satisfied me any more— I was simply under a cloud, even though I worked and slaved night and day. No matter what I tried, it was no use, my luck was gone.

A room on the second floor, the best guest room in the house, was where I was laboring away. I had been undisturbed up there since that first night when I had had plenty of money and could pay. I kept hoping, of course, the whole time that I would finish one of my articles and then be able to pay my room bill and whatever else I owed. That was why I was working so doggedly. I had one piece in particular I had started on and expected great things from, an allegory about a fire in a bookstore, a profound idea on which I intended to expend all my industry, finish it and bring it to the Chief in order to pay him back. The Chief would discover that this time he had really helped a person of talent; I hadn't the slightest doubt he would come to that conclusion; all I had to do was wait for the inspiration. And why shouldn't the inspiration come over me at any moment? My health was better now; I got a little food every day from the landlady, some bread and butter morning and evening, and my nervous state had almost disappeared. I no longer covered my hands when I wrote and I could look down into the street from my second-story window without becoming dizzy. I was much better in every way, and therefore I was a little surprised that I hadn't already finished my allegory. I didn't understand what the trouble was.

One day I got a glimpse of how weak I had really become, and how sluggish and incompetent my brain was. My landlady came up to my room with a bill which she asked me to look at—there must be something wrong with the addition, she said, her own accounts showed a different figure, but she could not find the error.

I sat down to add it up; my landlady sat facing me and watched. I added up the twenty or so numbers, first down, getting the same figure already there, and then up, and got the same result a second time. I looked at her; she was sitting waiting for my conclusion. As I glanced at her, it struck me that she was pregnant—that was clear to me, even though I hadn't looked at her for more than an instant.

"It's added correctly," I said.

"Would you check the entries then," she answered. "It can't be so much—I'm positive of it."

So I began to check every entry: 2 loaves of bread at

25 øre; 1 lamp glass, 18; soap, 20; butter, 32. . . . No particularly brilliant head was needed to go through these sums, this little uncomplicated grocery bill, and I tried hard to find the error she mentioned, but could not. After I had been grappling with these figures a couple of minutes, I felt them starting to dance around in my brain—I no longer made any distinction between debit and credit. I mixed them all up in one. Finally I came to a grinding halt at the following entry: 3 5/16 pound of cheese @ 16. My brain went click, and I stared dumfounded at the cheese, unable to go on.

"This is awfully squiggly handwriting!" I said in despair. "And right here someone has written, so help me God, five-sixteenths of a cheese. Who ever heard of anything like that—look here, you can see for yourself!"

"Oh yes," the landlady answered, "it's always written that way. That was some caraway cheese. It's right! Five-sixteenths works out the same as five ounces. . . ."

"Yes, yes, I know that!" I broke in, though in fact I couldn't understand a thing any more.

I tried again to get through this little exercise in addition which a couple of months ago I could have done in one minute. I sweated and concentrated with all my might on these enigmatic figures, and blinked my eyes thoughtfully as though I were making a real study of the matter, but I had to give up. Those five ounces of cheese finished me—it was as though something had broken in my brain.

However, to make it look as though I were still working on the bill, I moved my lips and now and then spoke some number aloud, and I moved my finger lower and lower in the column, as if I were making progress and would soon come to a decision. My landlady sat waiting. Finally I said, "I've gone over the whole thing from beginning to end and there is no mistake here, so far as I can see."

"You don't think so?" answered the woman. "No mistake?" But I saw clearly that she didn't believe me. And it suddenly seemed to me I noticed a faint tone of contempt in her speech, a note of indifference which I had not heard in her voice before. She said that I perhaps wasn't used to sixteenths; she said also that she would have to take the bill to someone more used to such work to get it really checked. She didn't say all of this in a wounding tone, to make me feel ashamed, but in a thoughtful and serious tone. When she got to the door and was about to leave, she said, without turning around, "Excuse me for having interrupted your work!"

She left.

Shortly after, she opened the door once more and walked in again—she must have gone no farther than the stairs before turning around.

"The truth is the truth," she said, "and you mustn't take it wrong, but don't you owe me something on your bill? You came, I think, three weeks ago yesterday? Wasn't that it? Making ends meet with a large family is not easy, so I can't let anyone live here on credit, I'm very sorry. . ."

I stopped her.

"I'm working on an article, as I mentioned to you before," I said, "and as soon as it is done, I will pay you everything I owe. You don't have to worry about that."

"Yes, but suppose you never finish that article?"

"I will. The right mood may come tomorrow morning, or even tonight yet—it's not at all impossible that the inspiration for it will come this evening, and then my article will be all done in a quarter of an hour at the most. You understand, with my work it's very different than with other people's—I can't just sit down and do so much every day. I have to wait for the right moment. And nobody can tell in what hour or day the inspiration will come! It has its own time."

My landlady left. But her confidence in me was clearly very shaken.

As soon as I was alone, I leaped up and started tearing my hair in despair. No, nothing would do any good for me, there was no salvation! My brain was bankrupt! Had I become completely a moron now since I couldn't even figure out the price of a piece of caraway cheese? But, on the other hand, could I ask myself questions like this if I were entirely witless? And besides all that, didn't I see, as clear as day, while I was struggling with the bill, that my landlady was pregnant? I had no way of knowing that fact, no one had mentioned anything about it, it hadn't occurred to me by association either, I was simply sitting there and saw it, and I understood it immediately, in the very same moments I was battling hopelessly with the sixteenths. How was I to explain that?

I walked to the window and looked out; my window faced on Vognmands Street. Some children were playing below on the cobblestones—poorly dressed children in the middle of a poor street. They were throwing an empty bottle from one to another with shrieks. A moving van rolled slowly by them—it must be an evicted family, since they were not moving at either of the two usual moving dates. That thought occurred to me the instant I looked. On the van there were bedclothes and furniture, worm-eaten bedsteads and dressers, chairs with three legs, painted red, rugs, ironworks, tin pans. A small girl, very young, an ugly child with a runny nose, was sitting on top of the load, holding on tight with her poor blue hands to keep from falling off. She sat on top of a bundle of frightful, stained mattresses that had been slept on by children, and looked down at the children throwing the empty bottle around. . . .

I stood watching all this and hadn't the slightest difficulty grasping what was going on. While I stood at the window taking this in, I also heard my landlady's hired girl singing in the kitchen, which was not far from my room—I recognized the tune, and I listened to see if she would make a mistake. I said to myself that an idiot could not have done all this, I was, thank God, in my right mind as much as anyone was.

Suddenly I saw two of the children in the street squaring off to fight, two small boys: I recognized one of them as the landlady's son. I opened the window to hear what they were saying to each other, and immediately a flock of children gathered under my window and looked up wistfully. What were they hoping for? For me to throw something down? Dried-out flowers, bones, cigar ends,

159

something or other they could chew on or play with? They looked up at my window with their little pale-blue faces and endlessly sad eyes. Meantime, the two diminutive enemies continued to hurl words at each other. Words like huge, cold-blooded reptiles poured out of their childish lips, frightful nicknames, whore language, sailor's curses which they had probably learned down at the wharf. They were both so taken up that they didn't notice the landlady who came storming out to see what was happening.

"You should see," explained her son. "He got me in the throat—I couldn't even breathe for an hour!" Then turning to the young evildoer who was standing smiling maliciously at him, he suddenly became wild with rage and shouted, "Go to hell, you blockhead, you Egyptian snot! A snotty louse like you grabbing people's throats! By God, I swear to hell I'll . . ."

And the mother, the pregnant wife who dominated the whole narrow street with her sheer size, said to the ten-year-old, taking hold of his arm to pull him along, "Shh! Hold your trap! Stop your swearing now! You sound as if you'd been brought up in a whorehouse! Shut up now and come in!"

"No, I won't!"

"Yes you will!"

"No, I won't!"

I stood at the window watching the mother's anger rising. This disagreeable scene had a strong effect on me, I couldn't stand it any longer, and I shouted down to the boy to come up here a minute. I shouted to him twice just to interrupt them and stop the wrangle. The last time I shouted very loud, and the mother turned and looked up at me bewildered. An instant later, she regained her control, gave me an insolent look, positively an arrogant look, and turned back to her son with a scolding remark. She talked loud enough so I could hear it, and said, "You should be ashamed of yourself, letting people see what a bad boy you are!"

I stood there taking in all this, and there was nothing, not even a single insignificant detail, that I missed. My attention was as keen as it could be, I breathed in every little thing sensitively, and thoughts occurred to me about each thing as it happened. So it was impossible that anything was wrong with my brain. How could there be anything wrong with it, in view of all this?

Listen now, I'll tell you something, I said all of a sudden, you have been going around long enough worrying about your brains, and troubling yourself about that —now let's have an end to that nonsense! Is it a mark of insanity to notice and observe details as exactly as you do? You almost make me laugh, that's the truth. There is something funny in this whole thing, there really is. Everyone fails once in a while, and they always fail precisely in the most simple problems: that doesn't mean anything, it's just chance. As I've said before, I'm just a hairbreadth away from bursting out laughing at you. About that grocery bill with its piddling five-sixteenths of rat cheese, because that's all it was—how ridiculous, a cheese with caraway seeds in it—as far as this absurd cheese is concerned, the brightest man in the world could easily stumble·over that—even the smell of cheese like that is enough to finish a man off. . . . I went on mocking the cheese unmercifully. . . . "No, give me something I can eat!" I said. "Give me, if you please, five-sixteenths of a pound of good creamery butter! That's more like it!"

I laughed feverishly at my own jokes and found them extremely amusing. There was really nothing the matter with me any more, I was in good shape.

My courage rose higher as I walked back and forth in the room talking with myself; I laughed aloud and felt wildly happy. It was as if all I had needed really was this little animated interlude, this moment of clear joy without a trace of sorrow, to get my head in working order again. I sat down at the table and started pushing my allegory forward. And it went very well, better than it had for a long time. The writing didn't go fast, but I felt the little I did do was absolutely first-rate. I worked on for an hour without becoming tired.

I was at an extremely critical point now in my allegory concerning a fire in a bookstore—it struck me strongly that everything that had come before was as nothing compared to this point. I wanted to give shape now to the really deep thought that it was not the books that were burning, it was brains, human brains, and I wanted to create a pure St. Bartholomew's Day out of these burning brains. Suddenly the door was thrown open and the landlady barged in. She walked right to the center of the room, without even pausing on the threshold.

I gave a hoarse cry—it was exactly as if someone had hit me.

"What?" she said. "Did you say something? We have a new guest and we must have this room for him. You can sleep tonight in the family room downstairs—you can have a bed to yourself." And before she had heard my answer she started gathering up my papers on the desk, getting them all mixed up.

My joyful mood was gone, I felt angry and depressed and immediately got up. I let her clear the table and said nothing—I didn't speak a word. She handed all the papers to me.

There was nothing for me to do, I had to leave the room, here was another precious moment spoiled! I met the new guest on the stairway, a young man with large blue anchors tattooed on the backs of his hands. Behind him came a longshoreman with a sailor's chest on his shoulder. The guest was without doubt a seaman, perhaps just a guest for one night; he probably wouldn't occupy my room any longer than that. Maybe I would be lucky again in the morning when the man was gone and get the inspiration back again—all that was lacking now was five minutes' inspiration, and then my allegory on the bookstore fire would be done. Well, there was nothing to do, fate was fate. . . .

I had never been in the family's own part of the house before—it was just a single room where they all lived night and day—husband, wife, the wife's father, and four children. The hired girl lived in the kitchen, where she also slept at night. With considerable aversion I approached the door and knocked. No one answered, though I heard talk inside.

The husband did not say a word as I walked in, did not even answer my greeting—he merely glanced at me with indifference, as if he had nothing to do with me. He was sitting playing cards with a man I had seen down at the pier—a dock worker whom people called "Glassy." An infant was lying on the bed gurgling to itself, and on a wooden settee bed an old man, the landlady's father, was sitting bent over, his head lowered over his hands as though his chest or stomach were hurting him. His hair was nearly white, and in his bent-over position he looked like a lizard with its head bent to the side, listening.

"I've come down here because I need a place to sleep tonight, I'm afraid," I said to the husband.

"Did my wife send you?" he asked.

"Yes. A new man has moved into my room."

To this the husband answered nothing—he went on with his card game.

The husband sat like this, day after day, playing cards with anyone who happened to come by; he played for nothing, merely to kill time and have something to keep his hands busy. He did not do a thing otherwise and moved only so much as he had to; his wife, meanwhile, trudged up and down the stairs, ran the house, and saw to it that the rooms were filled. She had connections with various longshoremen and dock workers whom she paid a certain commission for every new customer they brought her, and she often let these dock workers stay overnight besides. Tonight it was "Glassy" who had brought in the new guest.

Two of her children came in, a couple of small girls with thin freckled urchin faces; their clothes were pitiful. Shortly afterward the landlady came in also. I asked her where she wanted to put me tonight, and she answered curtly that I could sleep here along with everyone else or out in the hall on the settee, wherever I preferred. While she talked, she moved around the room, fussing with various things which she took care of, not once looking at me.

I lost my bravado at her answer; I stood by the door and tried to look small, and acted as if I were perfectly content to change my room for another for one night. I carefully put a friendly expression on my face so as not to provoke her and perhaps be thrown out of the house completely. I said, "Oh, this'll be fine!" and then was quiet.

She bustled around in the room still.

"By the way, I'll have to remind you that I simply cannot afford to let people have board and room on credit," she said. "I've told you that before also."

"Yes, you have, but it'll only be a couple of days now before I'll have my article done," I answered. "And then I will be glad to give you an extra five-kroner piece to boot, very happy to do it."

But she quite obviously had no faith in my writing, I could see that. On the other hand, I couldn't let myself be proud and storm out of the house only because of one tiny insult—I knew very well what was waiting for me if I left.

A couple of days went by.

I was sleeping in the family room; the hall had no stove and it was too cold there. I slept at night on the floor. The seaman was still living in my room and did not appear to be moving out soon. One noon the landlady came in and said the seaman had paid her for a whole month in advance; he was going to take a first mate's examination before he shipped out; that was why he was staying in town. As I listened, I understood that my room was gone for good.

I walked out in the hall and sat down. If I were to get any writing done, I would have to do it in the hall, where it was quiet. I was no longer excited by my allegory now —I had a new idea, a really marvelous plan: I was going to compose a one-act play, *The Sign of the Cross*, set in the Middle Ages. I had already thought out the main character thoroughly, a magnificent, fiery prostitute who had sinned right in the temple, not out of weakness or out of lust but from a sheer hatred of God, sinned right at the foot of the altar, with the altar cloth under her head, simply out of a delicious contempt for eternity.

I became more and more fascinated with this character as the afternoon went on. Finally she stood before me, living; all her characteristics stood out vividly. Her body would be deformed and repulsive: tall, extremely thin, and rather dark—and when she walked, her long legs would gleam through the fabric of her clothing at every step. She would also have large, protruding ears. In brief, she would be nothing much to look at, hardly bearable in that respect. What was wonderful about her was her marvelous lack of shame—the extra measure of deliberate and desperate sinning which she had done. She fascinated me almost too much: my brain was bulging with this rare monstrosity of a person. I wrote for two whole hours at a stretch on my play.

After I had finished ten, or perhaps twelve pages, all of which cost me considerable labor and were interrupted by wasted times when I went off on a tangent and had to tear the results up, I felt tired, almost stiff with cold and exhaustion; I stood up and went out to take a walk. For the last half hour I had been disturbed also by the children crying, so that I couldn't have written more just then anyway. I took a long walk along Drammens Street and was gone until after dark; as I walked along, I thought only of what would happen next in my play. While I was on that walk, I had this experience.

I was standing outside a shoeshop toward the bottom of Karl Johan Street, almost at the railway station market. God knows why I had stopped just outside this particular shoeshop! I was looking in through the window, though without thinking that I needed shoes; my thoughts were far off, in some other part of the world. People talking away walked past me, and nothing they said registered. Then a loud voice said, "Good evening!"

The one saying hello was Queeny.

"Good evening!" I answered in a distant way. I looked as Queeny awhile before I recognized him.

"Well, how goes it?" he asked.

"Fine, fine . . . as usual!"

"Listen," he said, "are you still at Christie's?"

"Christie's?"

"Yes, didn't you say last time that you were keeping the books for the Christie Foodstore?"

"Oh! No, that is finished. It was impossible to work with him—we separated by mutual consent."

"What happened?"

"Oh, I set down a number wrong one day. . . ."

"And he saw it, eh?"

Saw it? Queeny was implying right to my face that I had been cheating. He put in his question quickly; obviously he was very interested. I looked at him, felt deeply insulted, and did not answer.

"Oh well, Lord knows that can happen to anyone!" he said, to comfort me. He still believed that I had been fired for dishonesty.

"What is all this about Lord knows that can happen to anyone?" I asked. "Deliberately making a mistake? Do you really think I could do something as low as that? Me?"

"But, old boy I thought sure you said . . ."

I threw my head back, turned away from Queeny, and stared down the street. My eyes fell on a red dress which was coming toward us, it was a woman walking with a man. If I hadn't just had this conversation with Queeny, and hadn't been offended by his vulgar suspicion, and made this toss of my head, this red dress would likely have gone by me without my noticing it. And what concern was it of mine anyway? Suppose it was a lady-in-waiting at the court, what was that to me?

Queeny talked on and on, trying to retrieve his error; I didn't listen to him at all, I just stood there the whole time staring at this red dress coming closer. Something moved in my chest, I felt a delicate dart of pain—I whispered to myself without moving my mouth.

"Ylayali!"

Queeny turned around now too, noticed the couple, the woman and the man, raised his hat, and followed them with his eyes. I did not raise my hat, or maybe I did raise my hat. The red dress continued on up Karl Johan Street and disappeared.

"Who was that with her?" Queeny asked.

" 'The Duke,' didn't you see him? His nickname is 'The Duke.' Do you know her?"

"Yes, a little. Don't you know her?"

"No," I answered.

"It seemed to me you tipped your hat very elaborately."

"Oh, did I?"

"So you're not sure, eh?" Queeny said. "That's strange! What's more, you were the only one she looked at the whole time."

"Where did you meet her?" I asked.

"I don't really know her well at all. The thing was, it was one evening last fall. It was late, we were three lambs out on a spree, that sort of thing—we'd just left the Grand and we saw this woman walking alone, by Cammermeyer's Bookstore, so we spoke to her. She answered very coldly at first, but one of our party, a character not afraid of hell or high water, asked her right out if he could walk her to her door to make sure she got home safely, otherwise he wouldn't be able to sleep the whole night. He chattered constantly while they were walking, made up one thing after the other, swore his name was Waldemar Atterdag and that he was a photographer. Finally she herself had to laugh at this cheerful soul who hadn't been put off by her coldness, and it ended with him walking home with her."

"Yes, and what happened then?" I asked, holding my breath.

"What happened? Oh, come now! We don't ask that about a lady."

We were silent a moment, both Queeny and I.

"Well, I'll be, that was 'The Duke'! So that's what he looks like!" he said then, thoughtfully. "But of course if she is out with him I can't answer for her virtue."

I still remained silent. Yes, "The Duke" would obviously make the grade with her! So be it! What did that have to do with me? I said goodbye to her and all her charms: goodbye! I attempted to console myself by imagining the worst possible things about her, I took a positive pleasure in dragging her through the mud. The only thing that annoyed me was my taking off my hat to the couple, if

I had really done it. Why should I tip my hat to people like that? She meant nothing to me any more, nothing at all. She wasn't even the slightest bit beautiful to me, she had lost all her beauty, frightful, how ugly she had become! It wasn't out of the question that she had looked only at me—that wouldn't surprise me: she was probably feeling remorse now. But that didn't mean that I had to fall down at her feet, and bow and scrape like a fool, especially when she had clearly lost so much of her good looks lately. "The Duke" could have her then, and good riddance! Perhaps one day I would simply walk proudly right past her without even glancing in her direction. It wasn't impossible that I might do that even if she were to look straight at me, and what's more even if her dress were absolutely blood red! That could very easily happen! Yes, that would be a triumph! If I knew anything about anything, I would finish my play this very night, and within eight days I would bring that girl to her knees. Charms and all, yes, even with all her charms. . . .

"Goodbye!" I said curtly.

But Queeny pulled me back. He asked, "What do you do with yourself now during the day?"

"Do? I write, naturally. What else should I do? That is where I get my income. At the moment I am working on a great play, *The Sign of the Cross*, with a theme drawn from the Middle Ages."

"Heavens!" said Queeny, without irony. "If that gets produced . . ."

"Don't worry on that score, at all!" I answered. "In about eight days' time, I think you will hear a lot more of me."

With that I left.

When I got home, I went immediately to my landlady and asked her for a lamp. It was very important to me to have this lamp—I didn't intend to go to bed tonight, my play was racing through my head, and I hoped to write a great deal of it before morning. I presented my request in a very humble voice when I noticed that she made an irritated face just seeing me come in the door. I had nearly finished a remarkable play, I said; all that was lacking now were a couple of scenes, and I hinted that one theater or another would very likely perform it almost before it was finished. And if she would do me this great favor, I . . .

But the lady of the house had no lamp. She thought about it, but could not remember there being an extra lamp anywhere. If I wanted to wait until after midnight, maybe I could use the kitchen lamp. But why didn't I just buy a candle!

I didn't reply. I didn't have the ten øre for a candle, and she knew that very well. There I was, naturally, stuck again! The hired girl, in fact, was sitting in the family room now, just sitting there, and wasn't in the kitchen at all, so the kitchen lamp wasn't being used. I thought about all this but said nothing.

The girl suddenly turned to me.

"Didn't I see you leaving the Royal Castle an hour or so ago? You must have been there for dinner!" And she laughed at her joke.

I sat down, took out my manuscript, and was determined to work here anyway, right where I sat. I held the papers on my knees and stared firmly at the floor so as not to be distracted; but it was no good, I couldn't write a word. The landlady's two small daughters came in and started to tease the cat—a strange sick cat with almost no hair at all. When they blew into the cat's eyes, water poured from its eyes down over its nose. The landlord and a couple of other men sat at the table playing *cent et un*. Only the wife was, as usual, industrious; she sat sewing on something. She knew very well that I couldn't write in all this uproar, but she didn't bother about me any longer—she had even smiled when the hired girl asked about my whereabouts at dinnertime. The entire house had become hostile; it was as if it had taken only the single disgrace of my having to give up my room to another man for me to be treated exactly like an intruder. The hired girl, a little brown-eyed sluttish type with bangs and a flat chest, even made fun of me every night as I picked up my bread and butter. She never failed to ask me where I was in the habit of taking dinner, since she never seemed to notice me picking my teeth outside the Grand Café. It was obvious she was aware of my miserable circumstances, and enjoyed letting me know it.

I began to brood about all this suddenly, and I wasn't able to find a single speech for my play. I tried again and again; it was no use. My head started to buzz in a strange way, and I finally gave up. I put my manuscript into my pocket and looked around. The hired girl was sitting opposite me, and I gazed at her small back and her sloping shoulders, still half grown. Why should she attack me? And if I had been at the castle, what then? Could that have harmed her? She had been extremely impertinent lately, laughing at me whenever I happened to stumble on the stair or happened to get caught on a nail so that my coat ripped. And only yesterday she had picked up the first drafts of various scenes which I had thrown away in the corridor, actually had stolen these rejected fragments of my play, and had read them aloud in the family room, making fun of them in everyone's hearing, merely to amuse herself at my expense. I had never annoyed her and had never to my knowledge even asked her for a favor. On the contrary, I made my bed on the floor myself every night so as not to cause her any extra work. She made fun of me also because my hair was falling out. Strands of hair lay floating around in the washbasin every morning, and she made a great deal out of that. My shoes were by now in rather bad shape, especially the one driven over by the bread cart, and she found a few jokes there also. "God have mercy on you and your shoes!" she would say. Or: "Look at that shoe, it's the size of a doghouse!" She was right that my shoes were worn out, but I couldn't buy any others for the moment.

While I was sitting there brooding on this and pondering over the open enmity of the hired girl, the two small daughters started to tease the old man over in his bed. They both were hopping around him, completely absorbed in their entertainment. Each of them had straws which they were sticking into his ears. I looked on awhile and kept out of it. The old man did not move a finger to defend himself; he merely glared at his tormentors with furious eyes every time they poked him, and then shook his head to get free whenever the straws did get inside an ear.

I became more and more bothered by this teasing and could not take my eyes from it. The father looked up from his cards and laughed at the children's tricks; he called the attention of the other players to them also. Why didn't the old man move? Why didn't he throw the children aside with his arms? I took a step toward the bed.

"Let them be! Let them be! He's paralyzed," the landlord shouted.

Afraid of being turned out into the night, really afraid of angering the husband by mixing in this scene, I walked silently back to my old place and showed no emotion. Why should I risk my shelter and my bread and butter by sticking my nose into a family quarrel? No nonsense now for an old coot already half dead! I felt I was as deliciously hard as flint.

The little thieves kept on with their plaguing. It irritated them that the old man wouldn't hold his head still, and they began to jab for his eyes and nostrils also. He stared at them with a bitter expression, but said nothing; he could not move his arms. Suddenly he raised the upper part of his body and spit right into the face of one of the small girls; he lifted himself a second time and spit at the other too, but missed her. The landlord, as I watched, threw his cards down on the table and rushed over to the bed. He was red in the face and cried: "So you have the gall to sit there and spit in the eyes of children, do you, you old pig!"

"But, good God, they were torturing him!" I shouted, out of my mind. I didn't move from where I was; however, I was afraid of being thrown out, and I did not even shout with much force; my whole body shuddered from rage.

The landlord turned toward me.

"Now listen to him! What the hell does this have to do with you? Just keep your trap shut, and do as you're told —that's the best thing for you."

Now the landlady's voice rang out, and the whole house went into an uproar.

"God, if I don't think you are all crazy!" she shrieked. "If you want to stay in here, then you have to be quiet, both of you! Oh no, it's not enough that I have to keep house for bums and hoboes, I have to have people screaming as if they were in a madhouse besides! But I won't have any more of that, and that's final! Shh! Shut up, you kids, and wipe your noses, unless you want me to come and do it. I've never seen such people! Coming in out of the street without even enough money to delouse themselves, and the first thing you know, they are showing off in the middle of the night, fighting with the people who live in the house! I want no more of that, get that straight, and all those who don't belong here can go their own way. I want some peace in my own house, and I'm going to have it!"

I said nothing, I didn't open my mouth. I sat down near the door again and just listened. Everyone started to shout at one time, even the children and the hired girl, who tried to explain how the whole thing started. If I was quiet as a mouse, it would probably blow over—if I said nothing, the chances are it wouldn't go any farther. And what was I supposed to say? Wasn't it winter outdoors, and night on top of it? Was this the time to pound the table and fly off the handle? No idiotic tricks now! So I sat motionless and didn't walk out, even though I had been very nearly ordered out. I stared coldly at the wall, on which there was a colored lithograph of Christ, and kept my mouth obstinately shut during her raving.

"Well, if I'm the one you want to get rid of, that's all right with me," said one of the players.

He stood up. The other players stood up also.

"No, I didn't mean you. Or you two either," the landlady answered. "When I'm ready, I'll make it clear enough whom I mean. If I have to. It'll be clear all right. . . ."

She kept on talking, gave me these jabs at regular intervals and dragged the whole thing out so as to make it more clear to me that I was the one she meant. Silence! I said to myself. Just be quiet! She had not told me to go, not flatly, not in so many words, just no high-flown stuff on my part, no out-of-place pride! Just take it! . . . That colored lithograph showed a Christ with remarkably green hair. His hair was rather like green grass or, more exactly and precisely, heavy mountain grass. Yes, yes, a very sharp observation on my part, really, just like uncut mountain grass. .... A number of associations suddenly shot through my brain: from the green grass I moved to the Biblical saying about all flesh being like grass that is thrown into the furnace, and from there to the Last Judgment, when everything would be burned up, and then a little detour to the Lisbon earthquake, then I had a vague memory of a Spanish spittoon made of brass and a penholder made of ebony I had seen at Ylayali's house. Oh yes, it was all transitory! Just like grass thrown into a furnace! It all ended with four pine boards and a burial shroud—at Miss Andersen's, Main Entrance, to the right. . . .

All of this flew around in my head during those moments of despair when my landlady was just about to chase me out the door.

"He isn't listening!" she shouted. "I am telling you to get out of this house, now you've heard it! I swear to God I think this man is crazy! Now get out, right this minute, and no more gab about it!"

I looked at the door, I didn't want to go, I didn't want to go! A mad idea occurred to me: if there had only been a key in the lock, I would have turned it and locked myself in with the others; and then I couldn't have left the house. I had a dread of going out in the street that was positively hysterical. But the lock in the door had no key; so I stood up; all hope was gone.

My landlord's voice suddenly rang out over his wife's. I stopped, astounded. The man who had just threatened me was now, strangely enough, taking my side. He said, "You can't just throw people out in the street in the middle of the night. There's a law against it."

I didn't know if there were any law or not, I doubted it, but possibly there was. The wife had second thoughts, calmed down rapidly, and said nothing more to me. She even put two pieces of bread and butter in front of me for my evening snack, but I didn't take them—simply out of gratitude to the husband, I didn't take them; I said something about having had something to eat while I was out.

When I finally went into the hall to go to bed, the landlady followed me, paused on the threshold, and while her huge pregnant stomach jutted out toward me, said in a loud voice, "But this is your last night in this house, I want you to understand that."

"Yes, yes!" I answered.

It might be possible for me to find some rent money tomorrow if I put some thought to it. I would manage to get some sort of roof over my head. For the moment I was overjoyed not to have to leave tonight.

I woke about five or six in the morning. It was still dark when I woke, but I got up instantly anyway. I had slept in my clothes because of the cold in the hall, so I had no dressing to do. I took a drink of water, managed to open the door quietly, and left the house at once; I was afraid of meeting the landlady again.

The only things moving on the streets were one or two patrolmen who had been on duty all night; a little later, two men came along extinguishing the gas lanterns. I drifted about aimlessly, walked up to Kirke Street and then started down toward the fortress. Still cold and sleepy, my knees and back tired from my long walk, and extremely hungry, I sat down on a bench and dozed for a while. For three weeks I had lived on nothing but the bread and butter my landlady had given me twice a day; now a day had passed since I had last eaten; the ugly gnawing was beginning inside me once more, and I would have to do something soon. Thinking that thought, I fell asleep again on my bench. . . .

I was awakened by people talking nearby; when my eyes were open, I saw that it was bright day and everyone was up and walking around. I stood up and walked off. The sun blazed over the eastern hills, the sky was white and clear, and in my joy over the beautiful morning after so many dark weeks, I forgot my troubles entirely; I had been worse off before. I beat my chest with my fists and sang a few bars for myself. My voice sounded so rusty, its sound was so weak and pitiful, that I was moved to tears by it. The magnificent day, the clear sky overflowing with light moved me also, and I burst into loud sobs.

"What is the matter?" asked a man.

I didn't reply, just walked faster, hiding my face from people.

I walked down to the wharfs. A large ship flying a Russian flag lay at the pier, unloading coal. I read its name, *Copégoro*, on the prow. I was fascinated for a long time watching what was going on aboard the foreign ship. Although some ballast had already been taken on board, the ship must have been nearly empty, since I could read IX FEET on the depth scale painted on the side, and when the coal heavers walked over the deck with their heavy boots, the whole ship gave out a hollow sound.

The brilliant sunlight, the salt air from the sea, and all the busy and energetic movements gave me energy and cheered me up. All of a sudden it occurred to me that I might knock off a couple of scenes for my play while I was sitting here. I took out my manuscript.

I tried to compose a few lines for one of the monks, some sentences absolutely power-mad and stuffed with narrow-mindedness, but I couldn't do it. So I skipped the monk and worked on a long speech, the speech the judge delivers to the whore who violated the temple; I wrote a half page on this and then had to give up. I couldn't get the right tone in the language. All the workaday life around me, the loading chants, the noise of the winches, the constant rattling of the iron chains, was incompatible with the moody, self-absorbed atmosphere of the Middle Ages, which I wanted to be present in my play like a fog. I shoved my papers together and stood up.

Despite everything, I was really writing well, wonderfully, and I was positive I could accomplish a lot if I only had the right conditions. If I only had some place to go to! I thought and thought, stopped right in the street to think, but could not hit on a single quiet place in the whole city where I could hole up for a little while. There was nothing else to do, I would have to go back to the lodging house in Vaterland which I had just left. I winced at that, and kept assuring myself that this scheme would never work, but I kept on walking anyway and drew nearer and nearer to the forbidden spot. It was humiliating, certainly, I admitted it myself, degrading in fact, yes, positively degrading; but that didn't help either. Pride was not one of my faults; if I might make such a large generalization, I would say that I was one of the least arrogant creatures that had ever existed to date. I kept on walking.

At the street door I stopped and thought again. Well, well, whatever happened would happen, I would take the risk! But, after all, was this really such an important step as all that? In the first place, I would only be in the house a couple of hours, and second, I would never, as God was my judge, ever take refuge under this roof again. I started across the courtyard. Even while walking over the uneven stones of the courtyard I was still uncertain and nearly turned around. I clenched my teeth. No out-of-place pride now! If worst came to worst, I could always make the excuse that I had stopped in to say goodbye, and then take my leave after a conversation touching on my little debt to the house. I opened the hall door.

I stopped and stood still. Right in front of me, hardly two steps away, the landlord, coatless and hatless, crouched, peeking through the keyhole into the living room. He motioned to me silently to be quiet and peeked through the keyhole again. He was laughing.

"Come over here!" he said in a whisper.

I came on tiptoe.

"Look at that!" he said, laughing with a silent, convulsed laugh. "Take a look! Hee-hee! Look at them on the bed! Can you see old Grandpa? Can you see him?"

On the bed, right under the colored lithograph of Christ, and very close to me, I made out two shapes, the landlady and the new sailor; her legs showed very white against the dark quilt. And on the settee along the other wall was her father, the paralyzed old man, looking on, crouched over his hands, bent over as usual, unable to move. . . .

I turned back to my landlord. He had the greatest difficulty in keeping from laughing out loud. He held his hand over his mouth.

"Can you see Grandpa?" he whispered. "Oh God, can you see him there? Sitting there and watching!" He ducked down again to look in the keyhole.

I walked to the window seat and sat down. The glimpse of the two had brought my train of thought to an end, and my good mood was gone. But why should I care about all this? When the husband himself went along, in fact thought it great entertainment, why should I bother myself with it? As for the old man, well, one just can't worry about every old man. Maybe he couldn't even see, maybe he just sat there sleeping; God knows maybe he was even dead. It wouldn't surprise me at all if he were sitting there stone-dead. So my conscience could be left out of it.

I took out my manuscript again, determined to ignore all such distractions. I had broken off right in the middle of the judge's speech: "God and the Law tell me to do this, my council, myself and my own conscience tell me to do this; therefore . . ." I looked out the window, trying to figure out what his conscience told him to do. I heard a small sound from inside the living room. That sound had nothing to do with me, nothing whatever—the old man was dead anyway, he had probably died this morning about four; and I didn't give a hoot one way or the other about the sound. So then why in hell was I wasting time thinking about it? Be calm!

My self and my own conscience tell me to do this; therefore . . .

But everything was working against me. The husband at the keyhole did not keep still—every now and then I heard his suppressed laughter or saw him shaking; something was happening out on the street too that distracted me. A small boy had been sitting, playing by himself on the far sidewalk; he was playing peacefully, expecting no harm—fastening together some long strips of paper. Suddenly he jumped up swearing; he walked backwards out on the street, keeping his eyes on a grown man with a red beard who was leaning out of a second-story window, spitting down on his head. The child sobbed with anger, and, unable to do more, swore up at the window while the man laughed in his face—five minutes perhaps went by this way. I turned away so as not to see the boy sobbing.

My self and my own conscience tell me to do this; therefore . . .

I simply could not go farther. Finally, I couldn't see sense in any of it—even what I had already written looked useless, in fact the whole idea was ridiculous nonsense. One could not really talk about conscience in the Middle Ages: the inventor of conscience was that old professor of the dance, Shakespeare. My whole story, therefore, was unrealistic and false. Were all the pages worthless? I read them through again and changed my mind: I found wonderful places, long passages that were absolutely first-rate. I was overcome once more by the mad intoxication; I wanted to jump in and get the play done.

I stood up and walked toward the door, ignoring the landlord's angry gestures to me to make less noise. My mind made up, I walked out of the hall, up the stairs to the second floor, and into my old room. The sailor was not occupying it at the moment, that much was certain, and what harm was there in my sitting there a few minutes? I wouldn't touch any of his things, I wouldn't even use his table, just sit down on the chair near the door and be happy. I unfolded the pages hastily on my knees.

For several minutes the work went on swiftly. Speech after speech popped up in my head perfectly formed and I wrote on without a pause. I filled one sheet after the other, leaped over all obstacles, humming softly in delight over my rich mood. I was almost unconscious of myself. The only sound I heard during all this time was my own joyful humming. I got a new idea too, an excellent one, about a church bell that would suddenly burst out ringing at a certain point in the plot. Everything went marvelously.

Then I heard steps on the stairs. I shivered and almost leaped out of my skin; at that moment I was timorous, wary, afraid of everything, oversensitive from hunger. I listened nervously, held my hand and the pencil motionless, and listened—I couldn't write a single word. The door opened, the pair from the living room walked in.

Even before I had the time to say "Excuse me," the landlady cried, truly astonished, "Well, I'll be damned to hell if he isn't sitting here again!"

"I beg your pardon!" I said, and was about to go on, but stopped.

The landlady threw the door as wide open as it would go, and shrieked, "Now go! If you don't, God help me, I swear I will call the police!"

I stood up.

"I just wanted to say goodbye," I mumbled. "And so I've been waiting here. I haven't touched a thing, I've just been sitting on this chair. . . ."

"It's all right," the sailor said. "What the devil's the difference? Let him go!"

When I got to the bottom of the stairs, I suddenly became raging mad at this gross, swollen-up woman who was following on my heels to get me out as fast as possible, and I stopped an instant, my mouth full to the brim with hideous names I wanted to toss at her. But I reconsidered just in time and held my tongue, purely out of gratitude to the sailor who was coming along behind us and would have to hear it. The landlady followed me step for step, scolding at me all the time, while at the same time my rage grew with every step I took.

As we crossed the courtyard, I walked very slowly, still trying to decide if I should let go against the landlady. At this moment I was possessed by rage, and I thought of frightful acts of bloodshed, a blow that would knock her down dead on the spot, a kick in the stomach. A messenger in uniform passed me in the street door and said good morning; I did not answer. He turned to the landlady behind me and I heard him ask for me, but I didn't turn around.

A few steps beyond the door, the messenger caught up with me, greeted me once more, and stopped me this time. He handed me an envelope. I tore it open, unwillingly and hastily, and a ten-kroner note fell out of the envelope, but no letter, not a word.

I looked at him and asked, "What sort of nonsense is this? Who is the letter from?"

"I don't know, sir," he answered. "But it was a woman who gave it to me."

I stood where I was. The messenger left. Then I put the bill back into the envelope, crumpled the whole thing up in my fist, turned around, walked up to the landlady who was still peeping after me from the door, and threw the paper right in her face. I didn't say a thing, didn't utter a syllable, but I did wait to make sure she opened the crumpled paper before I left. . . .

That is what I would call the proper way to behave! Say nothing, not even write on the envelope, just quietly crumple it up into a big ball and throw it right between your enemy's eyes! There is an example of someone acting with dignity! That's exactly what they deserve, these animals!

When I got to the corner of Tomte Street and the railway station square, the street suddenly began to go around in circles, I could hear a hollow humming in my head, and I slumped over against a house wall. I simply could not walk any farther, couldn't even straighten up from my awkward position. I remained slumped over and felt myself beginning to lose consciousness. This attack of weakness merely strengthened my irrational rage, and raising my foot, I stamped as hard as I could. I also used various tricks trying to come to: clenched my teeth, wrinkled my forehead, rolled my eyes in despair, and it helped a little. My brain grew clearer, I understood that I was close to total collapse. I put my hands against the wall and shoved to push myself away from it. The street was still dancing around. I began to hiccup from fury, and struggled with every bit of energy against my collapse, fought a really stout battle not to fall down. I didn't want to fall, I wanted to die standing. A wholesale grocer's cart came by, and I saw it was filled with potatoes, but out of fury, from sheer obstinacy, I decided that they were not potatoes at all, they were cabbages, and I swore violent oaths that they were cabbages. I heard my own words very well, and I took the oath again and again on this lie, and swore deliberately just to have the delightful satisfaction of committing such clear perjury. I became drunk over this superb sin, I lifted three fingers in the air and swore with trembling lips in the name of the Father, the Son, and the Holy Ghost that they were cabbages.

Some time passed. I let myself sink down on a stoop and dried the sweat from my neck and forehead, fanned myself, and forced myself to calm down. The sun slowly sank, it was late afternoon. I began to brood over my situation again; my hunger was ghastly, and in a few hours it would be night; I had to find a solution while there was still time. My thoughts started circling again about the lodging house I had been evicted from; I absolutely did not want to return there, but I couldn't stop thinking about it. The landlady had been well within her rights, of course, in throwing me out. How could I expect to live in someone's place when I didn't pay! On top of it all, she had given me food now and then—even last night, after I had annoyed her, she had offered me two slices of bread and butter, just out of her goodness, she offered them because she knew that I needed them. So I had no complaints coming, and while I sat there on the stoop, I started asking and begging her forgiveness, silently, for my behavior. I especially regretted bitterly having shown myself ungrateful to her at the end, throwing that envelope in her face. . . .

A ten-kroner note! I gave a whistle. The letter the messenger brought—who had sent it? For the first time I thought about it and understood instantly how it all hung together. I became sick with shame and pain and whispered Ylayali several times in a hoarse voice, shaking my head. Didn't I only yesterday decide to walk proudly

181

past her when I met her and be utterly cold? What I had actually done was to awaken her pity and lure a little alms money from her. No, no, no, there was no end to my degradations! Not once in my relations with her had I ever been able to keep a dignified position—no, I sank every time, sank further, sank to my knees, to my waist, sank over my head in disgrace, and I would never come up again, never! This humiliation was the worst of all! Accepting ten kroner in beggar's alms without being able to throw them back to the giver, scrambling with both hands for coins no matter where they came from, and keeping them, using them for rent money even though one felt disgust inside. . . .

Wasn't there some way to get those ten kroner back? Going to the landlady and asking her to return the money would be useless, but there might be some other solution if I put my mind to it, if I just made a real effort and thought. In this case it wouldn't be enough, God knows, just to think in the ordinary way, I would have to make my whole body help me to look for a way to regain those ten kroner. So I sat down to think, and think hard.

It was probably almost four o'clock, and in a couple of hours I could go to see the Director if I had my play done by that time. I took out the manuscript and resolved firmly that I would finish the last three or four scenes; I meditated and sweated and read everything over from the beginning, but the speeches would not come. No rot now! I said, no hoity-toity stuff here! And I started to write blindly where I had broken off, I simply wrote down everything that occurred to me, just to get the play done in a hurry and get it over with. I tried to assure myself that I was experiencing a new creative mood, I lied to my own face, defrauded myself openly, and wrote on headlong as if I didn't even need to look for the right word. This is good! I've really hit on something here! I kept whispering to myself, just get it all down! But the last speeches I had put down began to seem suspicious to me finally—they were in such stark contrast to the earlier scenes, and there was nothing even remotely medieval about the monk's lines. I snapped my pencil off between my teeth, leaped up, tore my manuscript in two, ripped every page of it in shreds, threw my hat down on the street and jumped on it. "I am a lost man!" I whispered to myself. "Ladies and gentlemen, I am a lost man!" And I repeated that over and over as I went on jumping on my hat.

A policeman was standing a few feet away watching me—he stood right in the middle of the street, looking. When I raised my head, our eyes met—maybe he had been standing there a long time watching me. I picked up my hat, put it on, and walked over to him.

"Do you know what time it is?" I asked.

He waited a little before he hauled out his watch, and all the while he kept his eyes on me.

"Nearly four," he answered.

"Right!" I said. "Nearly four! Absolutely right! You know your job, I've seen that, and I won't forget you."

With that, I walked off. He was too astonished to speak, and stood looking after me with open mouth, still holding the watch in his hand. When I was about up to the Royal Hotel, I turned and looked back: he was still standing in the same position, following me with his eyes.

That's the way to treat these animals! With the most well-bred insolence! That impresses these animals, that puts the fear of God in them. . . . I was unusually pleased with myself and sang a few bars. Giddy with excitement, feeling no pain at all any more, feeling nothing at all unpleasant, I walked on, light as a feather, floated all around the market, curved around by the booths, and sat down on a bench near the Church of Our Saviour.

Did it really matter one way or the other whether I sent the ten kroner back or not? Once I had received it, it was mine, and certainly the house it came from was not hard up. I had to accept it, actually, since it had been expressly sent to me—there would have been no sense in letting the messenger keep it. There would be no point either in sending back a completely different ten-kroner note from the one I received. So there was nothing to do about it.

I tried to become engrossed in all the bustle going on

around me and occupy my thoughts with irrelevant details, but it didn't work and I kept coming back to the ten-kroner note. Finally I clenched my fists and got angry. It would wound her, I said, if I sent the money back—why in the world should I do it then? I always had to go around thinking I was too good for everything, shaking my head condescendingly and saying no, thanks. Now you see where that leads: here I am again tossed right out on the street. Even when I had the perfect opportunity to do it, I didn't hold on to my nice warm lodging house—no, I became proud, leaped up at the first word and started to pound the table, gave ten-kroner notes away left and right and walked out. . . . I scolded myself fiercely for having left my rooming house and so having drawn all this trouble upon myself.

For the money, damn the whole thing! The hell with it! I had not asked for that ten-kroner note and in fact I had hardly even held it in my hands—I had given it away immediately, paid off some total strangers I hadn't the faintest desire to see again. That's the sort of a man I am, I pay all my debts right down to the last øre. And if I knew Ylayali, she did not regret having sent me the money. Then why was I getting so worked up about it? Actually, the very least she could have done was to send me ten kroner now and then. The poor girl was in love with me, no doubt of that, maybe madly in love with me even. . . . I puffed myself up inside with this thought. There was no doubt—she was in love with me, the poor thing! . . .

It was five. I fell into depression again after my long stretch of nervous excitement, and began to hear the empty humming in my head again. I stared straight ahead, kept my eyes motionless, gazing off toward the Elephant Apothecary. Hunger was raging in me now, and I felt considerable pain. While I sat there staring down the street, a figure began to distinguish itself more and more from the background—finally it came perfectly clear and in focus and I recognized it; the cake seller next to the Elephant Apothecary.

I gave a start, sat up on the bench, and started to

think. All this had its own justice, that was the same woman in front of the same table in the same spot! I whistled once or twice and snapped my fingers, then I got up from the bench and started to walk toward the apothecary. No nonsense now! I didn't give a damn if those coins I gave her were from the devil's private stock, or good honest hunks of silver from the Kongsberg mine! Enough is enough, a man can die, you know, from too much pride. . . .

I walked over to the corner, took aim at the woman, and drew up in front of her. I smiled, nodded as though we were friends, and chose my words to give the impression that my return was very much a matter of course.

"Good afternoon!" I said. "Perhaps you don't recognize me this time?"

"No," the woman answered slowly. "I don't think I do." She looked at me.

I smiled still more, as if to say her not recognizing me was one of her rare little jokes. I said, "Don't you remember, I gave you a whole pile of kroner one day? On that occasion I said nothing, as I recall, I don't believe I did—I usually don't in those situations. When one is dealing with honorable people, I have found there is no need really to write everything down and, so to speak, sign a contract for every little thing. Ha-ha. Yes, I'm the one who handed you the money."

"Well, well, was that you! Yes, now I recognize you again, now that I think of it. . . ."

I didn't want her to start thanking me for the money, so I broke in quickly; my eyes were already roving over her table looking for something to eat. "Yes, and I've come now to get the cakes."

She didn't understand that.

"The cakes," I repeated. "I've come now to get them. In any case, some, the first installment, I won't need them all today."

"You've come to get them?" she asked.

"Yes, of course, I've come to get them, yes!" I answered and laughed loudly as though she should have realized a long time ago that I had come to get them.

As I did so, I picked up a piece from the table, a sort of French roll, which I started to eat.

When the woman saw that, she straightened up a little, made an involuntary movement to protect her goods, and said something to the effect that she had not expected me to return and rob her.

"No?" I said. "Oh, you hadn't?" Well, she was really a strange woman! Had anyone ever given her for safekeeping a walletful of money, and then not asked for it back eventually? Well, there, you see! I suppose she thought perhaps that this money was all stolen since I had thrown it down like that? No? She didn't think so? That was good! It was, if I might say so, very nice of her to give me the benefit of the doubt! Ha-ha! She was really a very good person!

"But why did you give me the money then?" The woman was exasperated and shouted that at me.

I explained why I had given her the money, and explained it calmly and precisely: I had a habit of conducting myself in this manner because I believed in humanity. Always, if anyone offers me a contract or an IOU, I shake my head and say, no, thanks. That is the way I am, it's true, so help me God.

But she still didn't understand it.

I had to adopt other means. I spoke in a sharp tone and said I wanted no twaddle. Hadn't anyone ever paid her in advance for goods just as I had? I asked. For example, people of means, people in the consular service for instance? Never? Well, I could not be responsible for the fact that she was unfamiliar with that procedure. It was perfectly ordinary procedure in other countries. Had she ever, by the way, been out of this country? No? Well, there, you see! She really had no right to an opinion in this matter. . . . I picked up several more cakes from her table.

She growled angrily, refused obstinately to turn over to me any merchandise she had on the table, even took one cake out of my hand and put it back in its place on the board. I became angry then, pounded the table, and threatened her with the police. I had tried to be easy with her, I said; if I took everything that belonged to me, I would absolutely clean her out, because what I gave to her that time was a really massive sum of money. But I didn't intend to take even as much as I deserved, I actually would accept half value. And I would never return again, to boot. God help us, that's the last thing I would ever do, seeing what sort of person *she* was.

Finally she picked out a few, naming an incredible price for them, four or five cakes, to which she tacked the highest price she could think of, and told me to take them and go. I went on arguing with her, complained that she had cheated me out of at least a kroner in the calculation and had absolutely robbed me blind with her fantastic prices. "Don't you know that there is a law against cheap tricks of that sort?" I said. "God have mercy on you. You could get slavery for life for that, you old bat!" She threw me one more cake and told me, almost grinding her teeth, to go.

So I left her.

"God, you'll never see anything to match a crooked cake seller!"

All the time while I was walking through the marketplace eating my cakes, I talked aloud about the woman and her disgusting behavior, repeated what we had said to each other—it seemed to me I had come out far superior in that exchange. I ate the cakes in full view of everyone as I went on talking.

The cakes disappeared one after the other. It didn't seem to matter how many I got down, I remained ferociously hungry. Why didn't they help! I was so greedy for them that I almost gobbled down the last cake of them all, which I had set aside almost from the start for the boy down in Vognmands Street, the small boy whose head the man had spit on. I thought of him all the time, couldn't make myself forget his face when he leaped up, crying and swearing. He had turned and looked toward my window, too, when the man spit on him, as if to find out whether I was laughing at him too. God knows, maybe I wouldn't even find him now! I hurried as fast as I could down to Vognmands Street, passing the spot where

I had torn up my play; some bits of paper were still lying there. I managed to avoid the policeman who had been so surprised at my behavior, and at last I arrived at the stoop where the boy had been sitting.

He was not there. There was almost no one on the street. It was getting dark and I couldn't see the boy anywhere. Maybe he had gone in. I put the cake down carefully on the threshold, leaning it up against the door, knocked hard, and ran off down the street. "He'll find it all right!" I said to myself. "He'll find it first thing when he comes to the door!" And my eyes grew damp over my idiotic joy at the boy finding the cake.

I walked back to the wharf area by the railway station.

I wasn't hungry any more, though the sweet food I had eaten was beginning to give me a stomach ache. Wild ideas popped up again in my head. What if I quietly went over and cut off the mooring ropes on one of the ships? What if I suddenly cried fire? I walked farther out on the pier, found myself a wooden box to sit on, and folded my hands; I could feel my brain moving nearer and nearer to chaos. I did not move this time, did absolutely nothing to prevent it.

I just sat there staring at the *Copégoro*, the ship with the Russian flag. I caught sight of a man at the rail; the red port lantern was shining down on his head. I stood up to speak to him. I had nothing in mind at all with my conversation, I didn't even expect to get an answer. I said, "Are you sailing tonight, Captain?"

"Yes, in a little while," he answered. He spoke Swedish. Probably born then in Finland, I thought.

"Hmm. You wouldn't need a man, would you?" I didn't care at that moment whether I got a no or not, it was all the same to me which answer he gave me. I waited, watching him.

"Oh, no," he answered. "We'd have to have a young man."

"A young man!" I straightened up, whipped off my glasses and put them in my pocket, walked up the gangplank and strode on board.

"I am inexperienced," I said, "but I can do whatever you give me to do. Where does this ship go?"

"We have ballast to Leeds. After that, coal to Cádiz."

"Good!" I said, pushing myself on him. "It makes no difference to me where it's going. I will do my job, and that's all I care for."

He stood awhile looking at me, thinking it over.

"Have you ever worked on a ship before?" he asked.

"No. But as I said, give me a job, and I'll do it. I am used to doing all sorts of work."

He thought it over some more. In my head I already saw myself going along, and I wanted badly to go; I began to be afraid he would chase me back on shore.

"What do you think, Captain?" I asked, finally. "No matter what job it is, I'll do my share. More! If I couldn't do more than my share, I would really be worthless. I can take two watches in a row if I have to. That would do me good, and wouldn't bother me at all."

"All right, all right, we can try it," he said, and smiled a little at my last words. "If it doesn't work out, we can always part company in England."

"Yes, that's right!" I answered, overjoyed. I repeated that we could always part company in England if it didn't work out.

So he gave me a job to do. . . .

When we were out on the fjord, I straightened up, wet from fever and exertion, looked in toward land and said goodbye for now to the city, to Christiania, where the windows of the homes all shone with such brightness.

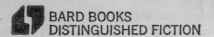

**BARD BOOKS
DISTINGUISHED FICTION**

Finally, in one paperback volume...the finest
writers in all of Latin America are represented
in an anthology which Jorge Luis Borges has
called *"quite impressive. All of the important
writers are there and the stories are all good...
Such a book will certainly be valuable...I know
nothing like it now."*

THE EYE
OF THE HEART
EDITED BY BARBARA HOWES

Outstanding short stories by Llosa, Fuentes,
García Márquez, Donoso, Borges, Asturias,
Amado, Cortázar, Paz, and thirty-three
others

20883/$2.25

BARD BOOKS

DISTINGUISHED FICTION

The Works of Thornton Wilder
America's Most Honored Writer

THE CABALA	24653	1.75
HEAVEN'S MY DESTINATION	23416	1.65
THE IDES OF MARCH	25213	1.75
THEOPHILUS NORTH	19059	1.75
THE WOMAN OF ANDROS	23630	1.65

 **BARD BOOKS**

the classics, poetry, drama and distinguished modern fiction

A SELECTION OF RECENT TITLES

FICTION

BILLIARDS AT HALF-PAST NINE Heinrich Böll	23390	1.75
THE CABALA Thornton Wilder	24653	1.75
THE CLOWN Heinrich Böll	24471	1.75
DANGLING MAN Saul Bellow	24463	1.65
THE EYE OF THE HEART Barbara Howes, Ed.	20883	2.25
HEAVEN'S MY DESTINATION Thornton Wilder	23416	1.65
HERMAPHRODEITY Alan Friedman	16865	2.45
THE MAZE MAKER Michael Ayrton	23648	1.65
THE RECOGNITIONS William Gaddis	18572	2.65
THE VICTIM Saul Bellow	24273	1.95
THE WOMAN OF ANDROS Thornton Wilder	23416	1.65

DRAMA

THE CHANGING ROOM, HOME, **THE CONTRACTOR: THREE PLAYS** David Storey	22772	2.45

POETRY

YEVTUSHENKO'S READER Yevgeny Yevtushenko	14811	1.45

Where better paperbacks are sold, or directly from the publisher. Include 25¢ per copy for mailing; allow three weeks for delivery.

Avon Books, Mail Order Dept.
250 West 55th Street, New York, N. Y. 10019

BC 7-75